Tell Me A Story At Christmas

Tell Me a Story at Christmas

Heartwarming Stories from Around the World

compiled by
Kathryn Deering

Vine Books
Servant Publications • Ann Arbor, Michigan

Vine Books is an imprint of Servant Publications especially designed to serve evangelical Christians.

The editors and the publishers express their appreciation for permission to reprint the stories and excerpts selected for this book. Every effort has been made to trace all copyright owners; if any acknowledgment has been inadvertently omitted, the publishers will gladly make the necessary correction in the next printing.

Published by Servant Publications
P.O. Box 8617
Ann Arbor, Michigan 48107

Cover illustration: Hile Illustration and Design, Ann Arbor, Michigan
Cover design: Diane Bareis

96 97 98 99 00 10 9 8 7 6 5 4 3 2 1

Printed in the United States of America
ISBN 0-89283-987-2

LIBRARY OF CONGRESS CATALOGING-IN-PUBLICATION DATA

Tell me a story at Christmas : heartwarming stories from around the world / compiled by Kathryn Deering.
p. cm.
Includes bibliographical references.
ISBN 0-89283-987-2
1. Christmas—Fiction. 2. Short stories. I. Deering, Kathryn.
PN6120.95.C6T45 1996
808.83'10833—dc20 96-3108
CIP

Dedication

To Mike
with gratitude for the first twenty-five years

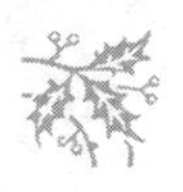

They all were looking for a king
To slay their foes and lift them high:
Thou cam'st, a little baby thing
That made a woman cry.

GEORGE MACDONALD (1824-1905)

Contents

Introduction / 9

Let Nothing You Dismay / 11
Ruth Harnden

A Father for Christmas / 19
author unknown

The Christmas Tree / 39
Mary Austin

A Long Way, Indeed / 51
Arvid Lydecken

The Tailor's Christmas Guest / 57
Marcel Brun & Betty Bowen

Teacher Jensen / 65
Karin Michaelis

A Memory of Stalingrad / 79
Joan Coons

A Carol for Katrusia / 93
Annie B. Kerr

What Amelia Wanted / 103
Elsie Singmaster

To Springvale for Christmas / 119
Zona Gale

Christmas Eve on Lonesome / 133
John Fox, Jr.

A Brand of His Own / 141
Harry C. Rubicam, Jr.

"I Gotta Idee!" / 165
Elsie Singmaster

Which of the Nine? / 181
Maurus Jókai

Christmas in the Cathedral / 191
Elizabeth Goudge

The Innkeeper / 211
Douglas Livingstone

Sources / 223

Introduction

Christmas. Something about it inspires story-telling. Perhaps it's the time of year. In the Northern Hemisphere, where so many of our holiday traditions have originated, December 25 falls during the cold, dark winter. Even in our climate-controlled homes and offices, we cherish cozy images of families and friends gathered hearthside for evenings of comfortable conversation and storytelling.

Perhaps also it's the "greatest story ever told" connection. In the bleakest season of the year, Christians celebrate the life-bringing story of Jesus' birth. We rejoice not only in our faith, if we are believers, but in the delightful paradox of it all: the supreme God of heaven and earth sent his only Son to be born in a barn. The scheme for human redemption is initiated not through grandiose utterances or compelling force—but through the birth of a baby in the middle of winter.

Tell Me a Story at Christmas is a collection of stories from the United States and Europe,written as early as 1904. Despite the wide variety of settings, characters, and plots, you will notice a common thread throughout the book; the old Bethlehem story is hiding between the lines of story after story. It often makes the worldly-wise stumble, this message of redemption through humble love and sacrifice.

May we all, in our individual everydayness, provide unwritten testimony to the same message.

Kathryn Deering

Let Nothing You Dismay

Ruth Harnden

. . . We can be so sure that every detail
in our lives of love for God is
worked into something good.

ROMANS 8:28, *THE MESSAGE*

She had spent the afternoon trimming the tree. She had trimmed it after the fashion of her native land, with bright-red, polished apples hanging, for balance and for beauty, under each pure-white candle. The old customs, her distant youth, were sharp in her memory. Sometimes they were sharper than the events of her present life in this New England village where she had come so many years ago and raised her American family.

Sometimes, and more often of late, she would find herself forgetting things that happened only the week before. She would make confusing mistakes, answer letters she had answered already, or else forget to answer them at all. It surprised her very much. She could remember so brilliantly every tree in her mother's garden, every street in the small Swedish town where she had grown up, every face and name of her early playmates and neighbors. It was very puzzling.

She sat now in the dark room, in the fragrance from the balsam tree, and watched the year's first snow falling beyond the window. She would not light the candles yet. She was saving them for the

children. If the snow kept up, she knew it would make the walking bad. But she hoped that it would keep up. She found it beautiful—and more than that. She had never lost, or perhaps she had found again, a childlike sense of magic in the presence of the first snowfall.

How strange it must be, she thought, to live where there is always snow. There was Hilda in the mountains of Oregon—Hilda who had cooked for her so faithfully until she married that crazy miner and went to live in some shack in the wilds. So *cold,* she would write in her letters. *Always so cold it is, I think I never be warm again.*

Rocking gently in the warm room, smelling the Christmas tree, watching the quick, feathered air outside, she thought with satisfaction of the socks she had knitted for Hilda. Six pairs, extra heavy. Hilda's feet, at least, would be warm.

She had mailed them in plenty of time. Last week, wasn't it? And there was still a week to go before Christmas. But then, she asked herself abruptly, what was it that she had mailed this morning? Something to Hilda, she was sure. She remembered thinking of her at the post office this morning, and she had written on the wide, flat box—but that was impossible! That was the box from Martins. That was the nightie for Janie, who was getting married right after Christmas.

15

Her granddaughter getting married! Only think. It was hard to realize. And it was the loveliest nightie she could find, the color of honeysuckle and trimmed with real lace. "Extravagant," she told herself dutifully now, but it didn't prevent her from smiling. It was so beautiful, and so was Janie—and she was getting married. Nineteen. Janie was nineteen. It didn't seem possible. And she had sent the nightie this morning to...

She stopped the gently rocking chair and sat straighter, trying to stop her thoughts until she could straighten them.

She had stood at the table in the post office, under the placard listing the states and their mailing dates—"For Florida," "For Oregon"—and she had thought of Hilda. "Oh, dear!" she said aloud, because now she could remember very clearly writing "Mrs. Hilda Borge," writing the Oregon address. "And the socks?" she asked herself. Had she sent the socks to Janie in Florida? But she could write to Janie. She could explain. It was of Hilda that she needed to think.

For a moment she was seeing the plain and practical Hilda with an awful clarity, because she was seeing her in relation to the bridal nightie, the gleaming satin, the cobweb lace. It was a picture so incongruous as to be almost indecent. And no one would be quicker to know that than Hilda herself. How she scorned all softness, all luxury and beauty, outside of the protective shell she

had built around her own poverty and plainness. "Such nonsense!" she could hear Hilda saying. "When so many are hungry and cold." But it was really the beauty that Hilda feared, as though she had to deny its existence or she would have to admit her own deprivation—her small, middle-aged, shapeless body, her homely work-scarred hands, the hopeless plainness of her face. She was unredeemed by a single beauty, and the only wonder was that even the thickheaded, bowlegged miner had wanted to marry her.

Would Hilda ever understand that it was only an old woman's fumbling mistake and not an insult, not a mockery to send that exquisite gossamer nightie into her poor stark shack where, in all likelihood, she slept in her long woolen underwear? Or would it break her heart with its terrible contrast with her own ugliness, its terrible reminder of all the luxury and loveliness that had no place in her own life? "How could I?" she asked herself. "And for Christmas, too?" The happiest time of the year, the time for remembering old friends with love and with loving gifts.

Even now in the distance, but still distinctly, she could hear the carol singers lifting their voices on the sharp and snow-filled air. "God rest ye merry, gentlemen, let nothing you dismay…" How ironic the words seemed to her now, like a rebuke to her shameful stupidity, her cruel blunder.

17

It was only the day after Christmas that she had Janie's wire from Miami—Janie who was so young and impatient, and too busy with her wedding plans to sit down and write a letter. *Marvelous ski socks,* the wire read. *How did you guess where we were spending our honeymoon?* So, that, at least, was all right, even though she had forgotten, after all, to write an explanation to Janie. Now she was glad that she hadn't written. Ski socks, indeed! It made her think of her own youth in Sweden, and it was a number of minutes before her mind returned to the present. But then she *had* sent the nightie to Hilda! For a little while, for a few happy Christmas days, she had forgotten.

It was another week before Hilda's letter came. *Old Hilda,* it began (in the middle of her own thought, after the habit of her simplicity). For a second she thought her worst fears had been realized, and her heart shook. But her eyes moved rapidly on. *Old Hilda, they think, there is only to keep her warm. So they send the sweaters, the mittens, the socks. What could make her pretty, such a one, eh? But you, my lovely friend, you have the other heart, the other eyes, and I am beautiful now! I open up the tight-air stove so the room is full of heat, and I put on my beautiful dress made for dancing, and what you think! I dance! Old Hilda dance, can you think of it? And my Tim he come and dance with me. Ha, I think my Tim he fall in love with me all over again.*

A Father for Christmas

Author unknown

Each person is given something to do
that shows who God is: Everyone gets
in on it, everyone benefits. All kinds of
things are handed out by the Spirit,
and to all kinds of people!
The variety is wonderful.

1 CORINTHIANS 12:5-6, *THE MESSAGE*

Sheriff John Charles Olsen let out a sigh so hefty it blew an apple core clear off his desk. There'd been times in his life when he'd felt worse. The night he'd spent in the swamp behind the Sundquist place with a broken leg and about a million mosquitoes for company was one such time. But there'd never been a time when he'd wanted less to be a sheriff.

"Are you deaf?" Mart Dahlberg demanded.

Sheriff Olsen looked across at where his deputy was typing out letters in his usual neat and fast way. "Did you say something?"

"Only three times. Didn't you promise the fellow you'd be out there by noon?"

"It ain't noon yet."

"It will be by the time you get there."

Sheriff Olsen hauled himself, slow and heavy, to his feet.

"Sure you don't want me to go along?" Mart asked, and his voice was gentler sounding.

The sheriff shook his head. "No, not much stuff out there. "Just four chairs and a table and the kids' clothes and some bedding."

"Well, I wish you'd get started," Mart said, "You got to be back here and into your Santa Claus outfit by three, remember."

22

"I haven't forgotten," the sheriff answered. He sounded snappish, but he couldn't help it.

Mart got up from his desk. "Look, John," he said, "take it easy. Folks get evicted from their homes all the time."

"Not a week before Christmas, they don't," the sheriff growled.

He slammed shut the office door and went out of the courthouse to where his car was parked. He gave a quick look at how the trailer was fastened, then he got into the car and slammed that door shut, too.

Maybe it wasn't anybody's fault what had happened. But it made the sheriff feel awfully queer in his stomach to have to move three little kids out of their home just before he was going to dress up in a Santa Claus outfit and hand out gifts to other kids at the annual Christmas celebration!

Sheriff Olsen started up the engine and turned on the heater. Then he turned it off and wiped the sweat off his forehead with his mitten. Likely a man with more brains than the sheriff could have fixed things right for Stephen Reade.

Sam Merske called Stephen Reade a deadbeat and a phony, but that was because Reade hadn't made a good tenant farmer. Two years ago, when Reade had rented the farm from Merske, Merske had called Reade a fine, upstanding personality.

Sheriff Olsen had argued for months with Merske about Reade and the kids, figuring that all Reade needed was another summer to get things going right. But Sam Merske was a businessman and he expected his farm to produce and make money for him. Finally he'd taken Reade to court.

23

After that, the sheriff had done his arguing with Judge Martinson, but the judge said that Sam Merske had been very generous and patient with Reade, and that it was understandable Sam's wanting to get a competent man settled on his farm before spring came.

"This man, Reade," the judge had said, "is obviously not fitted to farm. That has been proven to my satisfaction, not only by his inability to make his rent payments but also by the condition the county agent tells me the farm is in. Let us not fog our judgment, John, with undue sentimentality. It will be far better for both Reade and his children if we face the issue squarely."

It wasn't Stephen Reade's fault what had happened. You have to be kind of raised to it to know what to do when your cow takes sick or the weather mildews your raspberries. All his life since he was a kid, Reade had been in the selling business in New York City, going from door to door, first with magazine subscriptions, and then with stockings, and finally with vacuum cleaners. It took hard work and brains and a lot more courage than the sheriff himself had to go around ringing doorbells and asking strange women to buy things from you. But Stephen Reade had sold enough to support a wife and three children.

After the third child was born, Mrs. Reade had been sick all the time. She'd been raised on a farm in Oregon, and she figured living in a big city was what made her sick. So when she knew she wasn't going to live, she'd made her husband promise he'd take the kids to the country.

Reade had promised faithfully, and after his wife was gone he'd

taken what was left of their savings and headed for Oregon. He'd gone as far as the bus depot in St. Paul when he'd read an ad. The ad had said that anyone with initiative and enterprise wanting to rent an A-one farm should apply to Sam Merske, proprietor of the Merske Dry Goods Store in Minnewashta County.

Sam had demanded three months' rent in advance, and that was all he'd ever gotten out of Reade. The cow and the chickens had taken all the leftover cash that Reade had, and the cow hadn't lived very long.

Johanna Olsen, the sheriff's wife, had bought all her eggs off of Reade for two months. After that, for another two months she'd bought as many as Reade had to sell. And, after that, there weren't enough hens left to give the Reade youngsters an egg each for their breakfasts.

The plan was to move the Reade family into the two empty rooms above the Hovander Grain and Feed Store. It wasn't a permanent arrangement, because Hovander didn't like the idea. "Eight days is all they can stay. I ain't no charitable institution, and I wouldn't do the favor for nobody but you, John."

But the eight days would get the Reade kids through Christmas.

Sheriff Olsen brought the car and the trailer up alongside the farmhouse. There was a big railed-in porch running around three sides of the house and you could see how a widower with three children would have liked the looks of the porch the minute he saw it—forgetting how hard a big old house was to heat.

The sheriff knocked at the door. After a minute he heard someone running and then Ellen's voice said, "Robbie don't go near

that door; I'm supposed to answer." In another minute, the door opened a crack.

Sheriff Olsen said, "'Lo, Ellen."

Ellen said, "Hello, Mr. Olsen," but she didn't smile back. "My father's out for the present, but you're welcome to wait in the kitchen. It's warmest there."

Sheriff Olsen sat down on one of the four chairs pulled up to a card table. On the table was a bundle tied up in a blanket; near the back door was a barrel covered with newspapers, and three suitcases fastened with ropes.

The sheriff said, "You sure been busy."

"I helped with everything," Robbie said.

Ellen said, "The stove belongs to Mr. Merske, and so do the beds and the clock. But the chairs and the table are all paid for and so they belong to us."

Sheriff Olsen looked at the clock. "Did your pa say when he's be back?"

"He's gone for something," Ellen said.

Robbie said, "Dad's gone to get us a surprise. Letty thinks he's buying her a doll, but Dad said what he's getting for us is heaps more important than anything you can buy in a store."

Sheriff Olsen smiled at Letty and she came over and put her head down on his knee. She was about four and she wasn't worried yet about how things were in the world.

When it got to be about half past twelve, the sheriff said, "Maybe we should all drive down the road a ways and give a lift to your pa!"

Ellen slid down from the window sill. "Are you getting restless, Mr. Olsen?" she asked.

26

"Kinda."

"Well, when you get awful restless, I'm supposed to give you a letter." She started toward the parlor door. Then she turned. "But first, you have to be awful restless."

"I am awful restless," he answered with a worried look on his kind face.

In half a minute, she was back with an envelope. Inside was a sheet of paper that had been written on with pencil:

> "To the Sheriff of Minnewashta County: I, Stephen Reade, being of sound mind and body, do herewith declare that I relinquish all legal claim to my three children, Ellen, Robert, and Letitia Reade. I do this as my Christmas gift to them, so that they may be legally adopted by some family that will take care of them. I herewith swear never to make myself known to their new parents. They are good children and will make their new parents happy.
>
> Yours very truly,
> Your grateful friend,
> Stephen Reade"

"Does it tell about my doll?" Letty asked, jumping up and down.

"Does my father say when he'll be back, Mr. Olsen?" Ellen asked. She was standing very straight at the sink, making little pleats in her dress. "Does he?"

Sheriff Olsen looked at the clock, and then at his watch. There'd be a freight train pulling out of the station in thirty-eight

minutes, and if Reade hadn't hitched a ride on a truck, he'd be waiting to bum one on the freight. But you couldn't chase after a deserting father with the fellow's kids in the back of your car.

"Does he?" Ellen asked again.

Sheriff Olsen gave a big hearty smile. "Well, what do you know about that? Your dad's changed his plans. He wants you should stay the afternoon with my wife. So, quick now, put on your coats and caps and boots while I unhitch the trailer."

"But aren't we taking our chairs and things, Mr. Olsen?" Ellen asked.

"I'll come back for 'em later. Where's your boots, Letty?"

"Mr. Olsen, I don't think my father would want us to leave without taking our furniture with us."

"Look, my wife's going to take you to the Christmas celebration and you'll get presents from Santa Claus and everything. Only we gotta hurry, see?"

"Daddy's getting me a present," Letty said.

Robbie shouted, "I think we'd better wait here for Daddy."

"There'll be a Christmas tree," the sheriff said, "and hot cocoa to drink and peanut butter sandwiches. Robbie, you got brains, see if you can find Letty's mittens. I got her boots here."

Next Ellen spoke up:"We aren't supposed to go to the Christmas celebration, Mr. Olsen. My father told us it's just for the children who live in town."

"Well, that's the big surprise your pa's got for you. Santa Claus wants the three Reade kids to be special guests. Letty, stick your thumb in the hole that was meant for your thumb in this mitten."

"I want my daddy," Letty squealed. "I want my daddy to take me to see Santa Claus."

28

"She's scared because Daddy isn't here," Robbie said. "Aren't you scared 'cause Daddy isn't here, Letty?"

Sheriff Olsen grabbed hold of Letty. "How good can you ride piggyback?" With that, he rushed her off to the car.

Going over the slippery road with the three children, the sheriff had to drive slowly and carefully back into town. Right away, when the sheriff honked, Johanna came running out of the house.

"Johanna, they haven't eaten yet. And could you please phone down to the Christmas committee and tell them that you're bringing three extra children so they will have time to get their gifts wrapped right."

Johanna opened the back door to the car, and the three Reade youngsters moved out toward the smile she gave them like they were three new-hatched chicks heading for the feel of something warm.

"Wow!" said Johanna. "Am I ever lucky! There's a whole big chocolate cake in the kitchen, and me worrying who was going to help to frost and eat it."

With the kids out of the car, the sheriff drove kind of crazy. Once he was past the courthouse and heading for the station, the traffic thinned out and there wasn't anybody's neck to worry about except his own.

The freight was in, and the sheriff drove straight up onto the platform. Lindahl, who was stationmaster, gave a yelp, but when he saw it was the sheriff, he yelled, "What's he look like?" and started running down the length of the train.

Sheriff Olsen headed east toward the engine, and found where somebody had once been crouching down in the snow on the embankment.

29

It was an open boxcar, and likely Reade had seen the sheriff already, but the sheriff called out Reade's name anyhow. Then he pulled himself up into the car.

It took half a minute for the sheriff to get used to the half light, but all that time Stephen Reade didn't move or try to get past him through the door. He just sat huddled up in his corner, pretending like he wasn't there.

Sheriff Olsen went over to him and put his hands under Reade's elbows and pulled him to his feet. Reade didn't say anything when the sheriff shoved him down off the boxcar into the snow. But when they were in the sheriff's car, the train gave a whistle and Reade said, in a whisper, "I was close to making it."

The sheriff drove around behind where the Ladies' Shakespeare Study Society had put a row of evergreens. He kept the heater going, and after a couple of minutes Stephen Reade stopped shaking some. The sheriff got out the vacuum bottle and poured coffee into its cap.

All of a sudden Reade gave a groan. "Let me out of here! For their sake, you've got to let me get away!" He started to rock back and forth, with his hands holding tight to his knees. "You've got to believe me! I'm no good for those kids! I've lost my nerve. I'm frightened. I'm frightened sick!"

For a long time the sheriff just sat next to Stephen Reade, wanting one minute to break the guy's neck for him, and the next minute to put his arm around him, and not knowing any of the time what was right to do.

After a couple of minutes he said, "A while back, you claimed I didn't know what it was like to be scared. Well, sometimes I get

scared, too. Take like this afternoon. This afternoon I got to dress up crazy and hand out presents to a whole roomful of kids. Last night I didn't sleep so good either, worrying about it."

Stephen Reade snorted.

"Well, it ain't easy like maybe you think," Sheriff John went on. "I have to get up on a platform, and all the kids'll be staring at me, and sometimes their folks come too."

"You certainly make it sound tragic."

"OK, if you don't figure it's so hard, you do it. I'll make a bargain with you. You be Santa Claus for me, and I'll find you a job. And while you're doing a good turn for both me and yourself, Ellen and Robbie and Letty will sure get a kick out of seeing their pa acting Santa Claus to all the kids in town."

For a long time Reade just sat staring through the windshield. Then he said, with his voice low and sober, "You couldn't find me a job. There isn't a man in the whole county who'd be half-wit enough to hire the loony that made hash out of Merske's farm. And you know it." Then he faced around to the sheriff. "But I'll play at being Santa Claus if you want me to. I've been owing you some sort of thanks for a couple of years."

Ten minutes later, the sheriff had Stephen Reade holed up in the washroom opposite his office. He pointed out where the outfit was hanging in the corner. "You better put the whiskers and cap on, too, while you got a mirror," he said, "I'll keep watch outside."

Sheriff Olsen closed the washroom door and stepped back almost into his deputy's arms.

31

"What you got in there?" Mart Dahlberg said.

"Stephen Reade. He's going to be Santa Claus."

"You crazy or something?" Mart asked. "You've been Santa Claus for five years. What you want to go and give your part to that dope for?"

"Look, Mart, don't yell. Reade's feeling awful low, see? Getting evicted and not having a job or nothing. And I kinda figured handing out the presents to all the kids would maybe pep him up some."

"The committee won't let him."

"The committee won't know until it's too late," the sheriff explained. "Maybe I figured crazy, but I had to figure something. And, anyhow, he promised his kids a good surprise."

Mart gave a gentle pat on the sheriff's back. "Well," he said, "I can pray for you, but I don't figure it will help much."

Twenty minutes later, Sheriff Olsen poked his head into the kitchen behind the church's big recreation room.

Mrs. Bengtson looked around from washing cocoa cups. "The eating's done with, John," she said. "And they're singing carols while they wait for you."

Sheriff Olsen said, "Thanks." He motioned Stephen Reade to slip past through the kitchen to the door that opened out on the little stage. Then he moved himself, quiet and unnoticed, around to the back of the recreation room.

The piano was playing "Silent Night" and the place was jampacked. The sheriff took off his hat and wiped his face. Then he sat down at the end of the bench that held Johanna and the three Reade kids. He smiled across the heads of the three kids at

Johanna, and then he closed his hand over the hot paw that little Letty had wriggled onto his knee.

Up on the stage the tree was a beautiful sight. It was nine feet tall, and the committee had decorated it with pretty balls, lights, and popcorn chains. Under the tree were the presents. The wrapping paper had all come from Merske's Dry Goods Store because this year Sam Merske was chairman of the committee and most of the presents had been bought at his store. Some of the paper was white and had green bells on it and some was red with white bells, and each bell had printed on it one of the letters of M-E-R-S-K-E. And they were a beautiful sight, too. But sitting next to the presents, low under the tree, hunched up like a discouraged rabbit, was Santa Claus.

Sheriff Olsen flattened his hat out on his knee. Mart had been right. Wearing a beard on his chin and putting stuffing over his stomach weren't going to put pep into Stephen Reade. All they were going to do was spoil the show for the children and make Reade feel more miserable even than before! Then the music stopped and the sheriff folded his hat in two. Mart had said he would pray and maybe he wasn't forgetting to.

All of a sudden a little kid down front squealed, "Merry Christmas, Santa Claus!" And after that, the whole room was full of loving squeals and chirpings and calls of "Hi, Santa!"

Stephen Reade straightened up his shoulders a bit and then he reached out a hand for one of the packages. Sheriff Olsen began to feel some better. At least, Reade was remembering what he was up on the stage for, and maybe the kids wouldn't notice that

33

Santa Claus didn't have his whole heart in the business.

Then a voice said, hoarse and angry, "Move over," and Sam Merske plunked himself down at the end of the bench.

Sheriff Olsen gave a low groan, and Merske said, "Surprised to see me, huh?"

"Kinda," the sheriff muttered.

"You got the nerve to be sitting here," Merske said. "Who you got up there behind those whiskers?"

Sheriff Olsen wet his lips and then he opened his mouth, figuring to say it was a friend. But Ellen Reade was quicker at opening hers. Ellen leaned over the sheriff's knees and lifted her face up, eager and excited.

"It's my father, Mr. Merske," she whispered. "Isn't he *wonderful?*" Then she gave a sigh like she was stuffed full of a good dinner, and turned back to stare at the stage again.

Sheriff Olsen stared at the stage too, but the tree and Santa Claus and the little boy who was getting his present were all blurred together because of the awful way the sheriff was feeling.

Sam Merske said, "So you put Stephen Reade up there in the whiskers and clothes and things that I supplied. Ain't that just beautiful?"

On the stage, a little girl was getting her package, and being a little girl, was remembering to say "Thank you."

Sam Merske said, "I'll get you for this. Putting a deadbeat up there to hand out stuff that's wrapped with my paper and tied with my string! A no-good loafer that'll ruin the whole show! A no-good—"

His voice was getting louder, and the sheriff stuck his elbow hard into Sam Merske's ribs to make him shut up before the Reade kids could hear what he was saying.

But just shutting him up for now wasn't going to help. There were an awful lot of ways Merske could shame Stephen Reade in front of his children—like taking away the table and chairs that Ellen had counted on belonging to her family.

Sheriff Olsen tried to swallow, but his mouth was too dry. His throat was dry the same as his mouth. But his face and neck were so wet it would have taken a couple of bath towels to mop them.

It wasn't just a dumb thing the sheriff had gone and done; it was a plain crazy thing.

"Look, Sam," the sheriff whispered, "I gotta talk with you outside."

"Not with me," Merske said. "I'm sitting right here until I can lay my hands personal on that bum."

"Crazy" was what his deputy had called the sheriff's scheme. But Mart Dahlberg had been kind and generous. "Wicked" was the word he ought to have used.

And then all of a sudden a little boy began to yowl.

"It's Johnny Pilshek," Ellen said. "He's mad 'cause Louie Horbetz got a cowboy hat and all he got was mittens."

Every year it happened like that. Two or maybe three or four kids would complain about their presents, and that was why the committee always hid half a dozen boxes of something such as crayons under the sheet to give them. But Stephen Reade didn't know about the extras, because the sheriff had forgotten to tell him.

Johnny Pilshek marched back up on the stage. He stuck out his

lower lip and shoved the mittens at Santa Claus. "I don't want mittens," Johnny howled. "Mittens aren't a real present."

Santa Claus took the mittens and inspected them. "Most mittens aren't a real present," he said, "but these mittens are something special. They're made of interwoven, reprocessed wool, Johnny. That's what the label says. And we had to order them especially for you at the North Pole, Johnny! Everywhere, boys have been asking me to bring them this special kind of mitten, but we haven't been able to supply the demand."

"I've got mittens already," Johnny muttered. "I don't want no more."

Santa reached out and took one of Johnny's hands and inspected it careful as he had the mittens.

"Certainly you've got mittens already, Johnny. But they aren't like these. Do you know why we had these made for you, Johnny? We had these made for you because your hands are rather special. You've got to keep those fingers of yours supple, Johnny. A baseball player, when he's your age, gets his fingers stiff from the cold, and what happens? He winds up in the minor leagues, that's what happens."

He put the mittens back into Johnny's hand. "And we don't want you in anything except the major teams, Johnny."

"Gee," said Johnny. Then he turned around and walked down off the platform, flexing the fingers of his right hand, slow and thoughtful all the way.

Sheriff Olsen let out the breath he'd been holding; he could see now how Stephen Reade had made a living for his wife and kids out of going from door to door with magazines and hosiery

and vacuum cleaners. The sheriff looked down at Ellen and Ellen looked up at the sheriff and gave a big smile.

"He sure *is* wonderful!" the sheriff whispered to her.

And then a little girl sitting next to Johnny Pilshek stood up and asked, solemn and polite, if she could bring her present back too. She'd wrapped it up in the paper again, and she kept it hidden behind her until she was up on the stage.

"I think it's a mistake," she said in an unhappy kind of a whisper. "What I got wasn't meant for a girl."

Santa took the package. "We don't often make a mistake, April," he told her, "but let's see." He opened the package up on his knees.

"I don't mind it's being a muffler," April said, "but that one's meant for a boy. I know, because it's just like one they've got in Mr. Merske's store in the boy's section for sixty-nine cents. And it's not one bit pretty, either."

Stephen Reade held up the heavy gray scarf. "You're right, April," he said, "This was made for a boy and it's not one bit pretty. All the same, we chose it for you. And here's the reason why. It was chosen especially to protect your voice."

"I don't care. I don't want to wear it."

"You're pretty, April, and someday you'll be even prettier. But this is a fact. To get into the movies or on TV you've got to have a pretty face, but you've got to have something else too. You've got to have a pretty voice, one that's been properly protected by"—he turned over one corner of the scarf—"by 40 percent wool, 60 percent cotton, vat-dyed."

37

He draped the thing over April's arm, and after a little bit, April began to stroke it.

"Should I wear it all the time, Santa?"

"No. Just when the temperature's below freezing, April. Have your mother check the thermometer every time you go out, and when it's below 32, then you wear it."

"Yes, sir—I mean, yes, thank you, Santa Claus."

Five minutes later, the lady who played the piano sat down again and started in on "Hark the Herald Angels Sing." On the stage Stephen Reade was standing up, singing, and motioning with his arms for everybody to join in. But the sheriff couldn't join in. He couldn't even open his mouth, let alone get any singing out.

Stephen Reade had done what the sheriff had asked him to, and he'd made a good job of it. And in return the sheriff had got Reade and his kids in a worse fix than ever.

The sheriff turned and looked at Sam Merske. He wasn't singing either—just scowling and muttering to himself.

The sheriff wet his lips. "Sam," he said.

Merske turned and glared. "So that was the gag," he said. "Pretty slick, pretty slick, arranging for him to give me a personal demonstration of his selling ability. Pretty slick."

"Huh?" said the sheriff, and when the song ended and the next one hadn't yet begun, he said, "Huh?" again.

"OK," said Merske, "you win this time. He gets the job."

"What do you mean?" the sheriff asked slow and careful. "You mean you're fixing to give Stephen Reade a job in your store?"

"With the competition I've got from the mail-orders, I'd give a shoplifter a job if he could sell like that guy can. He may not be a farmer, but he's a real salesman." Then he scratched at the top of his head and glared some more at the sheriff. "What gets me is that I never put you down for having either the brains or the brass to swing a deal like that. How'd you hit on it?"

Sheriff Olsen didn't answer. It would take an awful lot of talking to explain to Merske how sometimes things worked out fine even without any brains to help you. And, besides, the piano was getting started on "Jingle Bells," which was a tune the sheriff knew extra well.

Sheriff Olsen opened his mouth wide. He could tell from the way the folks in front turned around to frown at him that he was drowning them out. But he didn't care. There wasn't any better time than a week before Christmas, he figured, for bursting out loud and merry....

The Christmas Tree

Mary Austin

In the same way, any of you
who does not give up everything
he has cannot be my disciple.

Luke 14:33, NIV

Eastward from the Sierras rises a strong red hill known as Pine Mountain, though the Indians call it The Hill of Summer Snow. At its foot stands a town of a hundred board houses, given over wholly to the business of mining. The noise of it goes on by day and night—the creak of the windlasses, the growl of the stamps in the mill, the clank of the cars running down to the dump, and from the open doors of the drinking saloons, great gusts of laughter, and the sound of singing. Billows of smoke roll up from the tall stacks and by night are lit ruddily by the smelter fires all going at a roaring blast.

Whenever the charcoal-burner's son looked down on the red smoke, the glare, and the hot breath of the furnaces, it seemed to him like an exhalation from the wickedness that went on continually in the town; though all he knew of wickedness was the word, a rumor from passers-by, and a kind of childish fear.

The charcoal-burner's cabin stood on a spur of Pine Mountain two thousand feet above the town, and sometimes the boy went down to it on the back of the laden burros when his father carried charcoal to the furnaces. All else that he knew were the wild creatures of the mountain, the trees, the storms, the small flowering things, and away at the back of his heart a pale memory of his mother like the faint forest odor that clung to the black embers of

the pine. They had lived in the town when the mother was alive and the father had worked in the mines. There were not many women or children in the town at that time, but mining men jostling with rude quick ways; and the young mother was not happy.

"Never let my boy grow up in such a place," she said as she lay dying; and when they had buried her in the coarse shallow soil, her husband looked for comfort up toward The Hill of Summer Snow shining purely, clear white and quiet in the sun. It swam in the upper air above the sooty reek of the town and seemed as if it called. Then he took the young child up to the mountain, built a cabin under the tamarack pines, and a pit for burning charcoal for the furnace fires.

No one could wish for a better place for a boy to grow up in than the slope of Pine Mountain. There was the drip of pine balm and a wind like wine, white water in the springs, and as much room for roaming as one desired. The charcoal-burner's son chose to go far, coming back with sheaves of strange bloom from the edge of snow banks on the high ridges, bright spar or peacock-painted ores, hatfuls of berries or strings of shining trout. He played away whole mornings in glacier meadows where he heard the eagle scream; walking sometimes in a mist of cloud, he came upon deer feeding, or waked them from their lair in the deep fern. On snowshoes in winter he went over the deep drifts and spied among the pine tops on the sparrows, the grouse, and the chilly robins wintering under the green tents. The deep snow lifted him up and held him among the second stories of the trees.

But that was not until he was a great lad, straight and springy as a young fir. As a little fellow he spent his days at the end of a

long rope staked to a pine just out of reach of the choppers and the charcoal-pits. When he was able to go about alone, his father made him give three promises; never to follow a bear's trail nor meddle with the cubs, never to try to climb the eagle rocks after the young eagles, never to lie down nor to sleep on the sunny, south slope where the rattlesnakes frequented. Besides that, he was free to roam the whole wood.

When Matthew, for so the boy was called, was ten years old, he began to be of use about the charcoal-pits, to mark the trees for cutting, to sack the coals, to keep the house, and cook his father's meals. He had no companions of his own age nor wanted any, for at this time he loved the silver firs. A group of them grew in a swale below the cabin, tall and fine; the earth under them was slippery and brown with needles. Where they stood close together with overlapping boughs the light among the tops was golden green, but between the naked boles it was vapor thin and blue. These were the old trees that had wagged their tops together for three hundred years. Around them stood a ring of saplings and seedlings scattered there by the parent firs, and a little apart from these was the one that Matthew loved. It was slender of trunk and silvery white, the branches spread out fanwise to the outline of a perfect spire. In the spring, when the young growth covered it as with a gossamer web, it gave out a pleasant odor, and it was to him like the memory of what his mother had been. Then he garlanded it with flowers and hung streamers of white clematis all heavy with bloom upon its boughs. He brought it berries in cups of bark and sweet water from the spring; always as long as he knew it, it seemed to him that the fir tree had a soul.

The first trip he had ever made on snowshoes was to see how it fared among the drifts. That was always a great day when he could find the slender cross of its topmost bough above the snow. The fir was not very tall in those days, but the snows as far down on the slope as the charcoal-burner's cabin lay shallowly. There was a time when Matthew expected to be as tall as the fir, but after a while the boy did not grow so fast and the fir kept on adding its whorl of young branches every year.

Matthew told it all his thoughts. When at times there was a heaviness in his breast which was really a longing for his mother, though he did not understand it, he would part the low spreading branches and creep up to the slender trunk of the fir. Then he would put his arms around it and be quiet for a long beautiful time. The tree had its own way of comforting him; the branches swept the ground and shut him in dark and close. He made a little cairn of stones under it and kept his treasures there.

Often as he sat snuggled up to the heart of the tree, the boy would slip his hand over the smooth intervals between the whorls of boughs, and wonder how they knew the way to grow. All the fir trees are alike in this, that they throw out their branches from the main stem like the rays of a star, one added to another with the season's growth. They stand out stiffly from the trunk, and the shape of each new bough in the beginning and the shape of the last growing twig when they have spread out broadly with many branchlets, bending with the weight of their own needles, is the shape of a cross; and the topmost sprig that rises above all the star-built whorls is a long and slender cross, until by the springing of new branches it becomes a star.

45

So the two forms go on running into and repeating each other, and each star is like all the stars, and every bough is another's twin. It is this trim and certain growth that sets out the fir from all the mountain trees, and gives to the young saplings a secret look as they stand straight and stiff among the wild brambles on the hill. For the wood delights to grow abroad at all points, and one might search a summer long without finding two leaves of the oak alike, or any two trumpets of the spangled mimulus. So, as at that time he had nothing better worth studying about, Matthew noticed and pondered the secret of the silver fir, and grew up with it until he was twelve years old and tall and strong for his age. By this time the charcoal-burner began to be troubled about the boy's schooling.

Meantime there was rioting and noise and coming and going of strangers in the town at the foot of Pine Mountain, and the furnace blast went on ruddily and smokily. Because of the things he heard, Matthew was afraid, and on rare occasions when he went down to it he sat quietly among the charcoal sacks, and would not go far away from them except when he held his father by the hand. After a time it seemed life went more quietly there, flowers began to grow in the yards of the houses, and they met children walking in the streets with books upon their arms.

"Where are they going, Father?" said the boy.

"To school," said the charcoal-burner.

"And may I go?" asked Matthew.

"Not yet, my son."

But one day his father pointed out the foundations of a new building going up in the town.

"It is a church," he said, "and when that is finished it will be a sign that there will be women here like your mother, and then you may go to school."

Matthew ran and told the fir tree all about it.

"But I will never forget you, never," he cried, and he kissed the trunk. Day by day, from the spur of the mountain, he watched the church building, and it was wonderful how much he could see in that clear, thin atmosphere; no other building in town interested him so much. He saw the walls go up and the roof, and the spire rise skyward with something that glittered twinkling on its top. Then they painted the church white and hung a bell in the tower. Matthew fancied he could hear it of Sundays as he saw the people moving along like specks in the streets.

"Next week," said the father, "the school begins, and it is time for you to go as I promised. I will come to see you once a month, and when the term is over you shall come back to the mountain." Matthew said goodbye to the fir tree, and there were tears in his eyes though he was happy. "I shall think of you very often," he said, "and wonder how you are getting along. When I come back I will tell you everything that happens. I will go to church, and I am sure I shall like that. It has a cross on top like yours, only it is yellow and shines. Perhaps when I am gone I shall learn why you carry a cross, also." Then he went a little timidly, holding fast by his father's hand.

There were so many people in the town that it was quite as strange and fearful to him as it would be to children who have grown up in town to be left alone in the wood. At night, when he saw the charcoal-burner's fires glowing up in the air where the

bulk of the mountain melted into the dark, he would cry a little under the blankets, but after he began to learn, there was no more occasion for crying. It was to the child as though there had been a candle lighted in a dark room.

On Sunday he went to the church, and then it was both light and music, for he heard the minister read about God in the great book and believed it all, for everything that happens in the wood is true, and people who grow up in it are best at believing. Matthew thought it was all as the minister said, that there is nothing better than pleasing God. Then when he lay awake at night he would try to think how it would have been with him if he had never come to this place. In his heart he began to be afraid of the time when he would have to go back to the mountain, where there was no one to tell him about this most important thing in the world, for his father never talked to him of these things. It preyed upon his mind, but if anyone noticed it, they thought that he pined for his father and wished himself at home.

If drew toward midwinter, and the white cap on The Hill of Summer Snow, which never quite melted even in the warmest weather, began to spread downward until it reached the charcoal-burner's home. There was a great stir and excitement among the children, for it had been decided to have a Christmas tree in the church. Every Sunday now the Christ-child story was told over and grew near and brighter like the Christmas star. Matthew had not known about it before, except that on a certain day in the year his father had bought him toys. He had supposed that it was because it was stormy and he had to be indoors.

Now he was wrapped up in the story of love and sacrifice, and

felt his heart grow larger as he breathed it in, looking upon clear windless nights to see if he might discern the Star of Bethlehem rising over Pine Mountain and the Christ-child come walking on the snow. It was not that he really expected it, but that the story was so alive in him. It is easy for those who have lived long in the high mountains to believe in beautiful things. Matthew wished in his heart that he might never go away from this place. He sat in his seat in church, and all that the minister said sank deeply into his mind.

When it came time to decide about the tree, because Matthew's father was a charcoal-burner and knew where the best trees grew, it was quite natural to ask him to furnish the tree for his part. Matthew fairly glowed with delight, and his father was pleased too, for he liked to have his son noticed. The Saturday before Christmas, which fell on Tuesday that year, was the time set for going for the tree, and by that time Matthew had quite settled in his mind that it should be his silver fir. He did not know how otherwise he could bring the tree to share in his new delight, nor what else he had worth giving, for he quite believed what he had been told, that it is only through giving the best beloved that one comes to the heart's desire. With all his heart Matthew wished never to live in any place where he might not hear about God. So when his father was ready with the ropes and the sharpened axe, the boy led the way to the silver firs.

"Why, that is a little beauty," said the charcoal-burner, "and just the right size."

They were obliged to shovel away the snow to get at it for cutting, and Matthew turned away his face when the chips began to

fly. The tree fell upon its side with a shuddering sigh; little beads of clear resin stood out about the scar of the axe. It seemed as if the tree wept. But how graceful and trim it looked when it stood in the church waiting for gifts! Matthew hoped that it would understand.

The charcoal-burner came to church on Christmas Eve, the first time in many years. It makes a difference about these things when you have a son to take part in them. The church and the tree were alight with candles; to the boy it seemed like what he supposed the place of dreams might be. One large candle burned on the top of the tree and threw out pointed rays like a star; it made the charcoal-burner's son think of Bethlehem. Then he heard the minister talking, and it was all of a cross and a star; but Matthew could only look at the tree, for he saw that it trembled, and he felt that he had betrayed it. Then the choir began to sing, and the candle on top of the tree burned down quite low, and Matthew saw the slender cross of the topmost bough stand up dark before it.

Suddenly he remembered his old puzzle about it, how the smallest twigs were divided off in each in the shape of a cross, how the boughs repeated the star form every year, and what was true of his fir was true of them all. Then it must have been that there were tears in his eyes, for he could not see plainly: the pillars of the church spread upward like the shafts of the trees, and the organ playing was like the sound of the wind in their branches, and the stately star-built firs rose up like spires, taller than the church tower, each with a cross on top. The sapling which was still before him trembled more, moving its boughs as if it spoke;

and the boy heard it in his heart and believed, for it spoke to him of God. Then all the fear went out of his heart and he had no more dread of going back to the mountain to spend his days, for now he knew that he need never be away from the green reminder of hope and sacrifice in the star and the cross of the silver fir; and the thought broadened in his mind that he might find more in the forest than he had ever thought to find, now that he knew what to look for, since everything speaks of God in its own way and it is only a matter of understanding how.

It was very gay in the little church that Christmas night, with laughter and bonbons flying about, and every child had a package of candy and an armful of gifts. The charcoal-burner had his pockets bulging full of toys, and Matthew's eyes glowed like the banked fires of the charcoal-pits as they walked home in the keen, windless night.

"Well, my boy," said the charcoal-burner, "I am afraid you will not be wanting to go back to the mountain with me after this."

"Oh, yes, I will," said Matthew happily, "for I think the mountains know quite as much of the important things as they know here in the town."

"Right you are," said the charcoal-burner, as he clapped his boy's hand between both his own, "and I am pleased to think you have turned out such a sensible fellow."

But he really did not know all that was in his son's heart.

A Long Way, Indeed

Arvid Lydecken

translated by K.C. Pihlajamaa

Little children, let us not love in word or speech but in deed and in truth.

1 John 3:18, RSV

Snow lay heavy in the valleys and on the hillsides. Its white blanket covered everything in sight, and the branches of the spruce trees bent low under its weight.

It was a bright cold winter eve, and the fire blazed merrily in the Pakkasvaara cabin. But little Annikin was sick in bed with a high fever.

Mother was preparing supper. Father hadn't come home yet from work, nor had Ilmari returned from school. The school he attended was about six miles away. The road the young lad had to take was rough and desolate so that he actually needed all his strength to make his way home. However, this evening the skis worked well in the powder-like snow, and soon red-cheeked Ilmari stepped briskly into the living room of the cabin, after having first brushed off the snow in the storm shed.

"Good evening, Mother," he called, rushing over to Annikin's bedside. "How do you feel, Sister?"

Annikin opened her blue eyes, and a slight smile played over her features, but she was too tired to speak. Wearily her head sank back into the pillow and she, who was usually such a gay and cheerful playmate, slipped away asleep again almost immediately.

Soon Father, too, arrived, and they sat down to supper.

"Is Annikin asleep?" Father asked under his breath, turning his

head toward her bed. And when there was no reply, he continued: "It's too bad, but it just seems impossible to get money enough together to buy her the doll she wants so badly for Christmas."

"Oh, Father—can't you make it somehow?" Ilmari cried.

"I'm afraid I can't," Father sighed. "We'll be fortunate if we have enough to get through the winter."

As the days sped by, Ilmari kept on wondering how Annikin might yet get her doll. He was sure that, if she only could get it, joy would make her well overnight. A happy person simply can't be sick, he told himself.

The doctor was summoned. He left some medicine, but it didn't seem to do any good. And of course, Father had to pay the good man something, further depleting his funds.

Ilmari thought about it some more. The doll would be much better than all the medicines in the world. It would positively perform a miracle. He racked his brain to find a way to earn a little money. But there just wasn't anything because they lived so far out of town.

Christmas drew ever closer. Now there was only a week to go, and still Ilmari hadn't been able to think of anything profitable. In fact, the situation seemed quite hopeless. He was a small boy with limited strength; no one would want to pay him to do something even if he had lived near enough to try to find work. And times were lean everywhere in Finland.

At long last, however, he had a brilliant idea: he'd write the infant Jesus a letter! Since He was a child himself, He certainly

loved children and would understand how important it was that his sister get her doll. He sat down, poised his pen with determination, and wrote:

Dear Jesus,

I take my pen in hand to write you this letter. I need your help, because nobody else can help me. I am Ilmari and I live in the Pakkasvaara cabin. Annikin is sick. She is my little sister, five years old. She wants a doll for herself. But we can't buy her one because we're poor. If she only got the doll she would get well for sure. Dear Jesus, when you come to our place on Christmas Eve, please be sure to bring a doll. The Pakkasvaara cabin is six miles from the church in Siltasalmi. If you can only bring the doll I don't want anything for myself. And I will be grateful to you all my life.

Respectfully,
Ilmari

Christmas Eve had arrived. A lonesome candle burned on the table in the cabin and Father was reading from the Bible. Ilmari waited with bated breath for what would surely happen.

Suddenly there was a knock at the door.

"That's Him!" Ilmari cried.

But it wasn't Jesus at all. It was only the young doctor from town. He had come on skis and carried a heavy knapsack on his shoulders. That was the best way for him to carry his medical supplies.

He set the knapsack down on the wooden floor. After he removed his big mittens, he unclasped the fastenings. From inside, he drew a bag of coffee for Mother, and for Father some shining new money. For little Annikin, he had a lovely blue-eyed doll; she was quite beside herself with joy. Nor had Ilmari been forgotten. He received a book which gave him greater pleasure than he had ever known.

Never before had there been so merry a Christmas in the Pakkasvaara cabin! Annikin's doll proved a wonderful medicine, and she became better day by day.

But only Ilmari knew who had sent the doctor on Christmas Eve. No doubt, Jesus hadn't had the time to come himself. And besides, the way out to the Pakkasvaara cabin is a long one indeed....

The Tailor's Christmas Guest

Marcel Brun
and Betty Bowen

"I made known to them thy name, and I will make it known, that the love with which thou hast loved me may be in them, and I in them."

JOHN 17:26, RSV

Hundreds of years ago, when the hilltops of Northern France bristled with the turrets and battlements of great feudal castles, there lived a rich and handsome aristocrat named Gilbert de Maupertuis. In Lord Gilbert's castle, with its high donjon and its walls shining with arms and trophies, were a lively group of fashionable lords and ladies who lived only to amuse themselves, from sunrise to midnight, in an endless diversity of sports and pastimes.

Almost every day twenty stalwart knights, led by Gilbert himself, spurred their horses over the château's stout drawbridge and down the hill, their bright plumes and banners dancing and skipping about like the people of Avignon. Some mornings, accompanied by their giant mastiffs, they hunted; often they rode out to try their skill at some tournament given by a neighboring lord; just as often they galloped across the fields to storm the castle of a hostile nobleman.

Renowned Gilbert spurned no opportunity to gain even greater glory. Indeed, it was whispered that he sometimes waged war for no cause whatever. So great was the reputation of this gentleman and his knights for reckless daring, that his enemies no longer deemed it cowardly to hastily retire behind their moats

when they saw his banners approaching; rather it was thought prudent and wise.

Each day at sundown, tired but exhilarated, the heroes would return to Maupertuis to enjoy their customary evening of merriment and gaiety and to charm the ladies with their thrilling stories of adventure.

All was not happy-go-lucky mirth and gaiety among the tenants who lived in the little village below the castle. Often their fields were ravaged by brigandeering knights; sometimes their crops were destroyed and they were forced to live in dire poverty, with barely enough food to keep themselves alive through the winter months. They could bake their bread only in their master's ovens. They must marry whom their lord suggested. They must be forever willing to be called to his service. If they tried to escape, or dared to complain about their wretchedness, Lord Gilbert made his exactions even more rigid. Life in the village was very hard.

In fact, if it had not been for the good tailor, many of the commoners could not have survived. Old Jacquet was the only peasant on the manor toward whom Gilbert de Maupertuis showed any kindness at all. It was he who fashioned the fine clothes which were so important in gaining distinction for oneself. Indeed, Lord Gilbert de Maupertuis was sometimes called the most gorgeously dressed gentleman of all Western Europe. Jacquet was indispensable.

With the utmost humbleness, the tailor would venture to ask

little favors of his master, never selfishly, but always for those less fortunate than himself. He was the only one who could obtain the noble's occasional good will.

The great man used to visit his tailor often for fittings, and as Jacquet worked, he would amuse himself by shocking the poor old man with his blasphemous stories about the wickedness and impiety of the priests and the bishops and the archbishops. Poor Jacquet used to dread seeing Lord Gilbert after the nobleman and his knights had won a battle, or after he had jousted some unfortunate peer in a tournament.

Jacquet was an exceedingly pious man, and exaltation lent to the lord's mockery an almost unbearable keenness. "How strange it seems that the great King of Heaven, who has power over all mankind, was unable to save the Holy Land from the infidels!" proud Gilbert would exclaim. Many, many times, after his master had criticized the priests and the monks and the pope and even Christ or God himself, the poor old tailor would pray, begging the saints to remove the veil from his master's eyes, so that he, too, might feel God's divine presence.

One day the good tailor told his *seigneur* a little story: "My Lord," he said, "many years ago, Jesus returned to earth. Dressed in beggar's rags, he went from door to door to beg alms. The folk who received him well he blessed, and they lived afterwards in great happiness. But upon the heads of those who turned him away, Jesus placed a solemn malediction, and ever afterwards they knew only darkness and despair."

Of course, Lord Gilbert only laughed disrespectfully and mocked poor Jacquet. "Well," he said, with playful mercilessness, "if Jesus knocks at your door, *I* shall be willing to give him the most handsome suit of clothes *you* can make!"

Now it happened that His Majesty, King Philip, desiring to hear the holy mass of Christmas Eve at the famous Rheims Cathedral, sent a messenger to Lord Gilbert asking him for the night's lodging in his castle. His lordship felt extremely joyful and proud that such a great honor should be bestowed upon him.

In haste he cantered down the hill to his tailor's workshop to order the most splendid costume Jacquet could make. For almost an hour Lord Gilbert fingered and examined samples of costly velvets and satins of endless varieties, and finally decided that he would appear the most dashing in flaming red brocade. My, but it was going to be elegant! It was to be very snugly fitted, lined with pearly satin as soft as swan's-down, trimmed with luscious, rich ermine. The crowning touch was to be a mountainous ruff of Flemish lace, delicately fluted according to the latest style.

Jacquet had just two weeks to finish his master's beautiful Christmas suit. Hour after hour his diligent fingers busied themselves with cutting and stitching, hemming and pressing. Even late at night, lamplight peeked out from his shaded windows, which lent an air of mystery to this modest peasant so hard at work. The commoners decided that their kind friend was surely hiding something from them, and the buzz of gossip and specu-

lation grew louder and louder during those busy days before Christmas. What could he be making?

When Christmas Eve came, Jacquet helped his liege to don his new suit of clothes at his shop. A cluster of townspeople loitered about the door in anticipation. Jacquet heeded every particular, even to a careful sprinkling with costly Oriental perfume. The folk of the town, catching glimpses of scarlet and white inside, sniffed the air appreciatively.

Just as Lord Gilbert was leaving, Jacquet said quietly, "My Lord, I have something to announce to you. Jesus has knocked at my door. I have done as you said I should; I have given Jesus the finest suit of clothes I could make." Then the tailor pulled aside the curtain to his back room. There stood a man—horrors!—dressed exactly as his lordship was dressed! Every detail was identical: red brocade, lace ruff, ermine trimmings....

Lord Gilbert de Maupertuis drew nearer. In dreadful fascination he gazed at this other glorious aristocrat and recognized the poor rascal who begged alms near the gates of his castle. The men and women whispered and snorted with glee to see the richly dressed twins.

Suddenly, turning purple with rage, Gilbert seized his tailor by the shoulder. Jacquet felt no fear for himself—no, not even when his master raised a brocaded arm to box his ears. He stood very still, and only his eyes betrayed his soul, which was fervently praying, "Blessed Saint Peter, please, please. Help him to see Jesus!"

Something very strange happened. Lord Gilbert's arm dropped to his side; and as he turned away, it seemed as though a part of Jacquet's quiet patience had passed into his heart as well. "All right, I'll pay for it," he said slowly. Then he hustled out to his horse muttering, "Jesus! Jesus in that scamp of a beggar! Who could believe such a thing?"

So great was his preoccupation that Lord Gilbert was hardly aware of climbing to his saddle. As he rode along, his anger melted away completely, and all his efforts to call it back were in vain.

All of a sudden, halfway up the hill, as he looked up at the first Christmas Eve star, he understood why he felt so very meek and yet so sublimely happy. He knew he could never feel, as Jacquet did, that the rascal who had come to the shop door to beg for bread was Jesus himself; but deep down in his heart a voice was whispering to him over and over again that the Spirit of Jesus had been there, had been in that room, not in the poor beggar's body, but in his good tailor's heart.

Teacher Jensen

Karin Michaelis

"... I was in prison and
you came to visit me."

MATTHEW 25:36, NIV

If the school children had cared to look about them while they were playing hide-and-seek during recess, they would have seen the sharp tower of a mighty building piercing the air beyond a distant clump of trees. Unless you knew better, you would have believed that it was a castle where knights and beautiful ladies ate game off golden plates and on Sundays regaled themselves with macaroons. But the school children did know better. They knew, forgot, and remembered again, that it was a prison standing near them, where prisoners lived, each in his own cell, never seeing each other except at church, where black masks disguised their faces. They knew and forgot and remembered again.

Lauritz Thomsen belonged there. Not that he had done anything to be ashamed of—God forbid! But his father was the cook for the prison, and Lauritz knew what the prisoners got to eat—and what they did not get. He lived, so to speak, in prison, but apart from these men with the black masks. He was so accustomed to taking the shortcut across the fields to the high red wall and walking through the entrance portal, which was immediately closed and bolted after him, that it all seemed like nothing extraordinary. He could see it in no other light. But if his schoolmates began to ask him questions he would hold his peace and blush to the roots of his hair.

68

His mother worried and grieved about the prison, and sought as best she could to forget what was going on. Filling her windows with flowers, she tried to silence her unpleasant thoughts about the poor creatures breathing the deathly cellar air behind those iron bars. She laid by penny upon penny in the hope of saving enough to buy a little country inn, or any kind of establishment far away from the Living Cemetery, as the prison was called. During her dreams she cried aloud, waking her children, for she always saw people with black masks on their faces swarming behind walls and windows and threatening to kill her. Evil dreams arise from evil thoughts, it is said, but Frau Thomsen could have no evil thoughts. She had only once in her life gone through the prison. It still froze her with terror to think of it, and she could not understand how her husband could sing and enjoy himself at the end of his day's work. Nor could she comprehend how he could speak of the prisoners as if they were friends or comrades. When he began to carry on in this way she would leave the room and not come back until he had promised to talk about something else.

Children are children. They can accustom themselves to wading in a river where crocodiles sleep, or to playing in a jungle where snakes hang from the trees. Children become accustomed to living near a prison just as they get used to a father who drinks or a mother who scolds. They think of it, forget it, and remember it again. Thoughts glide across their minds like shadows; for a moment everything seems dark, and suddenly the sun shines once more.

Whenever a prisoner escaped the school children were thrown into a great commotion. They followed the pursuit from afar, listening to the

shots, the alarm signals, the whistles. They leaned out of windows and saw the prison wardens rushing in all directions, on foot and on horseback. Nothing was so exciting as a manhunt, either over winter snow or over green summer fields. When the fugitive was taken, peace descended upon all their souls. Now the only question was what punishment would be meted out to the victim, and all eyes were turned toward Lauritz. But Lauritz said nothing. He was ashamed without quite knowing why.

Prison and prisoners would be forgotten save when a boy or girl at play would suddenly gape at the high towers to the east, jutting up there above the forest.

The children had a new teacher. He was called Teacher Jensen—nothing more. If he had a Christian name, he was never called by it. Just Teacher Jensen. And Teacher Jensen was little and frail, and Teacher Jensen's voice was as little and frail as he. But there was a wonderful quality in his voice, like a violin that makes a much louder noise than anyone would believe possible.

The children did not sleep in his classes. They were not even drowsy. In his classes they forgot to write notes to each other or secretly to eat bread and butter behind their desks. They only listened and asked questions. Teacher Jensen had an answer for everything. They could ask Teacher Jensen all kinds of questions. But sometimes he would shake his head and say: "I seem to have forgotten it. Let me think a minute." Or worse yet: "I don't know. I never knew it. But I will look it up. It is to be found in some book, or a friend will tell me the answer." The

children found that there was something splendid about having a teacher of whom you could ask all kinds of questions and who sometimes did not know the answer offhand.

Teacher Jensen talked about new things and old, and his speech was not like pepper gone out from a pepper pot. Even while the children were playing in the fields, they would remember what he had said. Yes, it remained fast in their minds.

One day Teacher Jensen said that murder was by no means the worst thing a man could do, and that it was much worse to think or say or do evil to another human being, or to make a defenseless animal suffer. And the children were full of wonder. It seemed that a new door had been opened to them, and each passed through it, one after another. Yes, it was true, what he said. They understood his meaning clearly, but they cast their eyes down, for all of them knew they had often done what was much worse than murder. Perhaps they would do it again, but not willingly, never willingly.

One day Teacher Jensen brought with him a sick, whining little cat which he had found on his way to school. He had put it under his cloak to keep it warm, and he stroked its back and its sharp little head. It was an ugly, gray, dirty cat. Teacher Jensen did not tell the children what he was going to do with it, but simply sat with the cat in his lap and rubbed his cheek against its head. To the children this poor little sick gray cat was the whole world. They took a silent vow that they would cure it. Through Teacher Jensen's little gray cat they had peered deep into something beautiful and pure and alive.

71

Teacher Jensen often went on Sunday excursions with the children. Whoever wanted to could come, and all of them wanted to. It so happened that one Sunday afternoon in the autumn they were walking among falling leaves, and the earth clung to their shoes in little lumps. It had been raining, and was likely to rain again. Traversing a bit of open country, they soon entered the big forest in the distance. Ahead of them was the "castle" that was the prison. Lauritz ran in to get a scarf.

Teacher Jensen saw him and drew his hand over his eyes, and as he cast down his eyes it was clear that he had been crying; but no one asked anything, no one spoke. They arrived at a vast grove of fir trees standing in long rows, with their evergreen branches above and their yellow trunks below. Teacher Jensen explained that such a forest could grow from a mere handful of tiny grains. The children knew this perfectly well, yet it sounded quite new. They suddenly understood that trees lived and breathed, and that they strove for the light as poor people strive for bread.

"Now let's begin the game," said Teacher Jensen. "Let's imagine that this forest of fir trees is a prison, and that we are all prisoners, each in his own cell. Let us do this for one hour. I am holding a watch in my hand. During that hour let no one speak, for we are prisoners, and speech is forbidden."

This was a new game, a peculiar game. The rain had stopped some time ago, but drops were still falling from the high trees. The children stood, each under his own tree, and felt the water dripping and dripping on cheeks and hands. The children stood with the water dripping off them, laughing and shouting to each other side by side cell by cell.

Slowly the laughter died and their faces became serious. All eyes were directed toward Teacher Jensen, who stood with the watch in his hand. He seemed to see nobody, and did not announce when the hour should begin.

The children felt as if they ought to hold their breath, for surely something important and serious was afoot. It was not like the times when they had gone out with other teachers, when hatred and pride cropped up as soon as the school door was closed. This was serious, and each breath was like a bucketful of water from a deep, deep well. Was time standing still? Had not many hours already passed? Were they really prisoners after all?

They did not crawl away, although there was nothing to stop them. Teacher Jensen did not look around him at all, yet as soon as any of the children thought of creeping away they could not help remembering what happened when a prisoner escaped and they heard the shots ring out, the alarm bells clang, the whistles blow, and they saw the wardens riding off in all directions hunting the fugitive. Their feet would not obey them—they were bound fast by Teacher Jensen's word; the outstretched hand with the watch held them in their places. Yes, they were prisoners, each in his own cell, and darkness settled and a gentle mist descended, veil upon veil.

Was this what it was like being a prisoner?

The hour was up.

Everyone sighed with relief, yet they all stood quiet for a moment, as if they could not really believe that they had regained their freedom. They sprang up and clustered around Teacher Jensen, asking him ques-

tions. It was growing dark, and he put his watch in his pocket, saying: "It is just as hard to be a prison watchman as to be a prisoner."

The children had never thought of this before, and after a long pause Teacher Jensen added: "The lot of the prison warden is the hardest of all, for he can do nothing for the prisoners; and in his heart he wants to help them all he can, yet they are not able to read his thoughts."

And after another pause he said: "I knew a man who spent seventeen years in prison and then died there."

When Lauritz reached home his mother was sitting at the piano playing and singing. The smell of freshly baked cake filled the room. On the table stood a glass bowl of apples. Lauritz's father sat on a chair smoking his pipe. Without knowing just what he said or why he said it, Lauritz went up to the piano and whispered in his mother's ear: "When I am a big man I shall be a prison warden."

"What did you say?" she cried. "A prison warden, Lauritz? In there with those people? Never!"

Lauritz repeated: "When I am a big man I shall be a prison warden."

And then something happened that was never explained. Who had the idea first no one knew. Perhaps it entered all those little heads at the same time, in that hour when they were standing, each a prisoner under his own tree, each in his own cell—just in a single hour.

When Teacher Jensen was told about the plan, he only nodded as if he had known about it long ago. But when they begged him to talk to the prison inspector, since their scheme was contrary to all regulations, he shook his head, saying: "It's your idea. You must carry it out. It is up

to you, if you believe in yourselves, to stand fast by your beliefs."

That was two months before Christmas, and all the school children, big and little, boys and girls, were there. Money was the first necessity, and it had to be collected in modest amounts and earned in an honorable way. Teacher Jensen said that if the gift was not honest no good came of it. The children all saved the money that they would ordinarily have spent on sweets and on stamps for their albums. They went on little errands, chopped wood, carried water, and scrubbed milk cans, wooden buckets, and copper tubs. The money was put into a big earthenware pig that Teacher Jensen had put in the wardrobe at school. No one knew who gave the most or who gave the least.

Lauritz announced that, including the seventeen sick people, there were three hundred and ten prisoners in the jail.

In the middle of December the pig was broken and the money was counted over and over, but it did not amount to much. Then a little fellow came with his little private savings bank, and a girl with a little earthen receptacle in which she kept her spare pennies. That started them off. Many little hoardings destined for Christmas presents were emptied into the great common fund at school. See how it grew! Shiny paper was now brought, and flags and walnuts. Every day the whole school stayed until suppertime, cutting out and pasting. The little girls made white and red roses. They wove baskets, gilded walnuts, pasted flags on little sticks, and cut out cardboard stars, painting them gold and silver. The little ones made, out of clay, birds' nests with eggs in them, and little horses and cows that they covered with bright colors so they looked like real live animals. The boys cut out photographs and

made little boxes. With jigsaws they fashioned napkin rings and paper-weights.

Christmas trees were bought—three hundred and ten real fir trees, for which the gardener charged only twenty-five pfennigs apiece.

Teacher Jensen emptied his purse on the desk. It had once been black, but it had long since turned brown, and was full of cracks. "That belonged to the man who spent seventeen years in prison," he announced. "He had it there with him. He kept it there for seventeen long years."

No one asked who the man was, but the money had to be counted over many times, for the children's eyes were moist and they had to keep wiping the tears away.

On the Sunday before Christmas the children went with Teacher Jensen to the local store and bought a lot of tobacco and chocolate, almonds and raisins, playing cards and brightly colored handkerchiefs, and writing paper. And they got a lot of old Christmas books too, which were given to them free because they were at the bottom of the pile and were out of date.

The parents of the children had to contribute whether they wanted to or not, and bags full of cookies and nuts, playing cards and books, came out of each house.

Lauritz's father had spoken in all secrecy to the prison chaplain, who went as a representative to the inspector. But the inspector hemmed and hawed, saying: "That goes against all regulations. It's impossible. The men are not allowed the freedom to receive or keep anything. It can't be allowed on any ground whatever." The chaplain was to have

told this to Lauritz's father, and Lauritz was to have brought the news to the children that the plan had to be abandoned. But the chaplain said nothing to Lauritz's father, and the children did not know that it was impossible and could never be allowed.

All the parents, no matter how much they had to do, made a point of going into the schoolhouse the day before Christmas and seeing the three hundred and ten little sparkling Christmas trees, each laden with joy, each with its star on the top, each with its white and red roses, white and red flags, and white and red candles, each decorated with tinsel and hung with gifts. To every tree a little letter was fastened, written by a boy or a girl. What was in this letter only the writer and perhaps Teacher Jensen knew—for Teacher Jensen had had to help the little ones who only knew how to print numbers and capital letters.

The church bells rang over the town and called the faithful to God's worship. The prison bells rang out over the prison and called the prisoners to the prison church. Before the school was drawn up a row of wagons which had been laden with the little Christmas trees. Each child then took one of his trees under his arm and set out, following the wagons, singing as he went. It was a Christmas party without snow, but a Christmas party just the same.

Stopping before the prison, they rang the bell, and asked to speak to the inspector. He came out, and the moment he appeared Teacher Jensen and all the children began to sing: *"O du fröhliche, o du selige, gnadenbringende Weihnachtszeit...."*

The inspector shook his head sadly and raised his hands in the air. It was impossible, absolutely impossible—he had said so. But the children

kept right on singing, and seemed not to hear him. As the inspector afterward said, when the director of all the prisons in that district demanded an explanation: "A man is only human, and had you been in my place, Mr. Director, you would have done as I did, even if it had cost you your position."

Thus it came to pass that this one time Christmas was celebrated in each cell of the big prison—a good, happy, cheerful Christmas. When the prisoners came back from the worship of God with their black masks on their faces they found a Christmas tree in every cell, and the cell doors stood open until the candles had burned out, and the prisoners received permission to go freely from cell to cell all through the corridors to look at each other's Christmas trees and gifts—to look at them and to compare them. But each prisoner thought that his little tree and his present were the most beautiful and the best of all.

When the last light had burned out, the doors were closed, and far into the night the prisoners sang the Christmas carols of their childhood, free from distress, grief, and all spitefulness.

And as the last light flickered out behind the high walls the thin figure of a man with his coat collar up over his ears and his hat pulled over his face crept along the prison wall. Through the night air he heard the voices singing, *"Stille Nacht, heilige Nacht."*

Clasping his hands tightly together and raising them aloft into the darkness, he cried: "I thank you, father. Thy guilt has been atoned for ten times over."

A MEMO
STALINGRAD

Joan Coons

God chose the foolish things of the
world to shame the wise;
God chose the weak things of the
world to shame the strong.

1 CORINTHIANS 1:27, NIV

Her grandmother was dead. Nadia did not cry when the old women told her, nor was she afraid. She was sorry, of course, for she'd miss the stories her grandmother used to tell, but she was not afraid. Death was nothing to fear. Her father had told her that. Her mother was dead, as were many of the people she had known. No, death was nothing. There were worse things. The Germans were worse... trying to force their way into Stalingrad. Nadia listened. She could hear the distant roar of the guns, the thunder of bombs. The Germans were less than ten miles away.

"It is better to be dead," a woman muttered hopelessly. "When there is only fighting and bloodshed for the young, what can we old ones ask for?" She looked at the listening child, shook her head sorrowfully. "You're to sleep in my shack now," she said, turning away.

Nadia didn't answer. She was thinking of her grandmother. They'd put her in the farthest shack with the other bodies. There was no time for burials, no implements with which to dig a grave. Besides, the earth was frozen. The old women had kept Nadia

away from the shed, but she went there now, to say goodbye to her grandmother.

It was cold in the shed, but her grandmother would not mind. They were all cold… and hungry too. Nadia's father had said they should be glad of the cold, for it helped save Russia from the Germans. The Germans hated General Winter, as they called this deadly foe.

There was no odor of decay in the shed, for the cold had preserved the bodies. Later, the shack would be burned, with the bodies in it. But not now. They couldn't have any fires or lights that might attract the Germans. These scattered little shacks must be kept secret. Even the German planes had not discovered them, hidden there in the hills.

The Germans wouldn't bother with these shacks anyway, would dismiss them as the shelters of old people and children. And they'd be right; only they wouldn't know that here the great Russian flyer Petrovich met his comrades to discuss plans to save Russia. And Petrovich was Nadia's father.

"He's coming tonight," the child whispered to the dead about her. "My father's coming tonight." She drew close to her grandmother, touched the old woman's stiff face.

"It's Christmas Eve, you know," Nadia said wistfully, recalling the stories her grandmother had told her about the Christmas celebrations she'd known as a girl. That was in the old Russia, the Russia that had died, even as the grandmother herself had died. Nadia bent over the silent figure on the floor.

"He'll find you," she said softly, "I know He will." Her grandmother had believed the Christ Child came for the souls of the dead, and had been afraid He wouldn't find hers among so many dead and dying, afraid she would be overlooked and carried to the underworld by evil spirits.

Nadia sighed as she turned toward the door. She would not come again. It did no good to cling to the dead. Those were her father's words. She thought again of her father, pretended she was to buy him a present, and tried to decide what she would choose. Intent on these imaginings, she followed the trail into the hills, forgetting her father's rule that she must never go out of sight of the shacks.

Nadia came upon the light suddenly. A man had it, a stranger whose crouched figure was almost completely concealed by the ledge above him.

"Oh a fire!" she cried with pleasure, instinctively stretching out her hands toward it, and adding quickly, "Put it out!"

Startled, the man almost fell over. He hadn't heard her approach. His hand went automatically to the knife in his belt, stopped as the child spoke again.

"It's not allowed, you know," she said, fixing her eyes longingly on the candle where a moment before the man had been warming his cold hands.

The man did not reply. Fool that he'd been to stop! But who'd expect anyone here, especially a child? Now what was to be done with her?

"It's warm, isn't it?" Nadia said wistfully.

"Yes," the man replied, peering at her sharply. "Here, come closer and warm your hands a second. Then we'll put it out."

Nadia crept under the ledge beside him, held her hands cupped about the small flame, smiled at the man, the shy, appealing smile of a six-year-old.

"It's alive," she told him softly.

"Yes," he answered gruffly.

"It would make a lovely gift." She sighed. "Such a lovely Christmas gift."

The man reached over and pinched out the small flame. "A gift," he asked, "for whom?"

"My father."

"Oh." Still the man watched the child thoughtfully.

"He's coming tonight." Nadia paused. She'd been warned not to speak to strangers, most of all not to mention her father. But this man spoke Russian, not the hated German, and he was kind. He'd shared the candle with her. A German wouldn't have done that.

"Coming tonight?" the man asked, a sudden interest evident in his voice. "Coming," he repeated, "from where?"

The child leaned closer, her great dark eyes studied him for a moment. "From Stalingrad," she confided.

"No one can come from Stalingrad," her companion remarked shortly, without thinking. "The Germans will not let one escape."

"He will come," the little girl replied firmly. "The Germans cannot stop him. My father's Petrovich," she added proudly.

The moment the words were out, Nadia knew she had betrayed her father's secret. Quick tears filled the dark eyes. "You will tell no one?" she implored anxiously. "It's a secret. I shouldn't have told."

"It's all right," the man assured her. "Petrovich's meeting place is safe with me."

At the words "meeting place" Nadia looked up. Maybe the man knew all about the discussions held in the shacks. Maybe she hadn't given anything away after all.

"You know my father?" she asked hopefully.

"Yes," the other replied with fervor. "Yes, I know Petrovich."

Relief spread rapidly over the child's pinched little face. "Oh, it's all right then," she suggested eagerly.

"Yes, it's all right," he repeated, smiling at her. He picked up the candle, held it out to her. "A present," he said, "for your father, for Petrovich."

Nadia hesitated, intense longing in the dark eyes. The man was giving her the candle! It wasn't possible. No one gave away anything. People hadn't enough for themselves.

"Take it!" The man put the candle in her hand. "It's a magic candle," he told her.

"Magic?"

"In a way. You see," he explained, "it's been blessed."

"In a church?" Nadia interrupted. She held the candle carefully.

"Yes, in a church," he replied. "It will bring a blessing to the

house where it burns... and to those who sleep beneath the roof of that house. You must put it in the window tonight, after your father is asleep."

"Have you forgotten," the child reminded him, "we cannot have lights?"

"This is different," the man said sharply, added more gently, "A blessed candle on Christmas Eve lights the Christ Child to the door. No harm can come then... not even from the Germans." This last was uttered in a whisper, low, intense.

Nadia laid the candle against her cheek, remembering the warmth it had shed but a few minutes before. "You are kind," she murmured, "so kind... to give it to me."

"It is for Petrovich, the greatest flyer in all Russia."

That explained everything. Nadia smiled happily. The man had given her the candle because he loved her father. Everyone loved her father. All Russia loved Petrovich.

"But you must not tell your father about the candle or me," the man went on slowly. "The candle would lose its power if you did. You must tell no one. You must not speak of it at all."

"I know," she agreed. "The evil spirits might overhear and steal the blessing."

"Yes." The man lifted her back onto the path, watched her hide the candle beneath her shawl. "You must not say you have seen me... until tomorrow," he added hastily, seeing the surprise on her face.

"Tomorrow?"

"Yes... tomorrow I shall be with Petrovich," he told her slowly. "I'd like to tell him myself... about our meeting, I mean. I want to explain..." He broke off, smiled at her. Nadia smiled back. "Run along now," he told her, "before they miss you."

The child started down the path, stopped and looked back. "Goodbye," she said, waving to him.

"Goodbye," he answered. "Goodbye... little one."

"I'm Nadia," the child replied, turning away.

"Goodbye, Nadia," the man murmured, watching the little girl until she disappeared from view. He shrugged, muttered an oath, and started off into the hills.

The man stopped before the entrance of a cave, hidden by trees and almost buried under drifted snow

"I'm back, Karl," he called, stooping to crawl through the narrow opening. He spoke in German, and the man in the cave, the man called Karl, answered in the same tongue.

"I thought something must have happened to you... you were gone so long. Did you get a good look at the shacks, Hans?" he asked eagerly as the other came to sit beside him.

"Yes. They're the ones all right," Hans replied flatly.

"Good!" Karl was excited. "I was right. If only we knew when the next meeting..."

"Tonight," Hans put in abruptly.

"Tonight! How do you know?"

Hans smiled, but it wasn't a happy smile. He told Karl about the candle, the Christmas gift for Petrovich.

"It was a stroke of luck, our stumbling on this place," Karl said when Hans had finished. "It'll make it all worthwhile... all this." He glanced about the cave. "This hole... the days and nights we've lain here... waiting... waiting... and the cold..." He shivered. "Yes, even this damnable cold."

"We'll carry the gun to the hill above the sheds," Hans said tonelessly. "I found a good site this afternoon."

Karl touched the gun beside him. "We've only the one shell," he said, "but it won't be wasted now. They'd have found us sooner or later, and if they didn't we'd starve anyway." He shrugged. "The shacks are scattered. We could easily have picked the wrong one. There'd be no chance of a second shot... even if we had the shell," he added thoughtfully. "The first sound will bring every Russian in these hills after us." He paused, went on. "But we'll die knowing we brought down Russia's greatest flyer."

"Do you mind dying, Karl?" the other asked, thinking how young the boy was, not more than twenty at the most.

"Mind?" Karl's voice was vibrant. "Death is nothing," he said. "I would prefer to live to serve our leader and Germany, but I die to protect the Fatherland. It is my duty!"

"My duty," Hans muttered softly, under his breath. "It was my duty, little Nadia. Can a child like you understand that?"

"What are you mumbling about?" Karl asked impatiently.

"Nothing."

"I don't understand you sometimes," the boy began, but Hans interrupted him.

"We'll go as soon as it is dark," he remarked.

"Are you sure she'll light the candle?" Karl asked, doubtful for a moment.

"Yes," the older man assured him quietly. "I'm sure Nadia will light the candle."

Nadia held the candle in her hand, anticipating the warmth the small flame would give. Her father and his companion had sent her out while they talked, but now they were all asleep in the straw in the loft of the large shed. The men, posted to watch, would pay no attention to her. Nadia smiled to herself.

She hesitated a moment. The man's words came back to her. "It's a blessed candle. No harm can come."

Nadia slipped into the shed, struck the flint she carried. A few seconds later she was on her way to the old woman's cabin where she was to sleep. Pausing, she looked back at the lighted candle, pleased by the bit of flame.

"There it is!"

From the top of the hill, Karl peered through the sights of the gun, finding the range carefully, precisely. It had been a struggle, getting the gun there, making no sound that might carry to the people below. Time and again they had stopped, scarcely daring to breathe, fearing they'd been discovered.

"Ready," Karl said at last, then, as Hans did not answer, made no move, "What is the matter with you?"

"You're sure it's set?" Hans asked instead of replying.

"It's set," the boy said coldly. "It's not much of a light, but I found it."

Hans slid the shell in silently, peered through the sights briefly, then moved his hand mechanically. The sound of the exploding shell burst into the night. The aim had been perfect. A real blaze replaced the tiny flame of the candle.

Nadia stood by the blackened ruins of the shed the next morning. The Germans were dead, both of them, and her father was already on his way to safety. He'd left as soon as the explosion awakened him, not waiting to help put out the fire. There were other men to do that. Petrovich was needed for greater things.

Nadia sighed. Her father had been angry at first, when she'd told him about the candle, but afterwards he'd understood. She turned at the sound of a footstep behind her.

"Whatever made you do it, child?" the old woman asked, going to Nadia, pulling the child to her comfortingly.

"He said it was a blessed candle," the little girl replied, "that it would light the Christ Child to the door." Tears rolled down her cheeks, sparkled on the front of her shawl.

"But why did you change your mind and put it in this shack?"

the other asked, then added, "though it's a blessing you did."

"Grandmother was so worried that the Christ wouldn't find her soul when there were so many," Nadia explained. "I thought my father wouldn't mind if I put the candle in her shack instead of his." She sobbed as the old woman led her away from the charred timbers.

A Carol for Katrusia

Annie B. Kerr

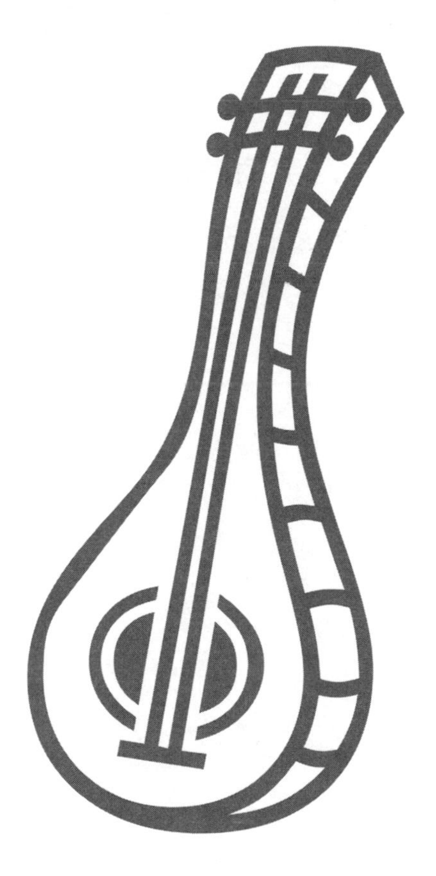

"Then the nations that are left round about you shall know that I, the Lord, have rebuilt the ruined places, and replanted that which was desolate; I, the Lord, have spoken, and I will do it."

Ezekiel 36:36, RSV

From the tiny kitchen of the Vincents' apartment delicious odors floated out into the narrow court and were wafted away over the snowy roofs of the tenement houses.

Mrs. Vincent sank down on Peter's cot in the dining room and went over in her mind the various items of the Christmas preparations. Her name wasn't Vincent at all, but the children, especially Catherine, had persuaded her several years ago that the name Vincent was much more sensible and practical than their real name, "Vinnichenko." She had, however, stubbornly refused to part with her first name, Katrusia, in spite of the children's objections.

From Peter's cot, where she was resting, Katrusia could see a little patch of gray sky through a lacy veil of falling snow. She loved the snow; it reminded her of the far-off steppes of Russia, of bells and sleighs and herself tucked inside a beautifully woven wool *kilim,* speeding through the frosty night. It reminded her of her Cossack father, stamping the snow from his heavy boots before he entered the house, and of her Cossack lover, riding across the plain from the next village where he lived.

Her eyes turned from the window and the falling snow to the

picture on the wall of the bride and groom in Ukrainian peasant attire. Twenty-five years ago that picture had been taken in Kiev, when Katrusia was just seventeen and Vanka twenty. Where was he now, that strong young Cossack, lost these twenty years? Every day she had asked herself that question. Every day during all the weary time in America she had watched for the boat to bring him back to the little family he had sent out from war-torn Russia. Every day she had watched for the letter that never came. Christmas time always brought him to her mind with renewed vividness, for five gay and happy Christmases had they spent together, walking through the snowdrifts at midnight to kneel side by side in the village church and pray at the manger crib of the Christ Child.

Indeed, it had been at a Christmas Eve celebration that she had first seen Vanka, the tallest and handsomest of all the village boys, singing the *Kolyadky* from house to house. His eyes had smiled boldly into hers, and he had bent low over her outstretched hand which held a coin, as he sang:

Yuletide wakes, Yuletide breaks,
Woman, give me eggs and cakes.

The two girls burst noisily into the room, interrupting their mother's reveries. They dropped their clumsy bundles on the floor and drew the gloves from their cold fingers. *"There,* Mamusia." Olga leaned down and rubbed her glowing cheek

against her mother's pale one. "We've searched the whole neighborhood for this straw and wheat. It's grand outdoors, just like your old Russia."

Catherine stooped to untie the bundle. "A nice mess we'll have in the house," she pouted.

Katrusia sighed and got up from the cot, the remembrance of days long ago still in her eyes. She and Catherine had had a long and bitter conflict over this Christmas celebration.

"We're American—why should we celebrate Christmas on January seventh, and spend days beforehand cooking more food than anybody can eat?" Catherine had protested.

"Because we're Ukrainians first—before we are Americans—and because we have church on January seventh and not on December twenty-fourth and twenty-fifth, even here in America," Katrusia had replied. But Catherine was not to be persuaded. She was spoiled, was Catherine, the baby of the family. Russia and Russian ways meant nothing to her. At her age Katrusia was already married, with Catherine in her arms and Peter and Olga clinging to her skirts.

It was really Peter who had saved the day. Peter, who was always looking out for someone less fortunate than himself; Peter, who when just a little boy had assumed the responsibility of the family.

"Just one more time we shall have a Ukrainian Christmas," Peter had decreed. "I've found two homesick fellows over at Levitsky's rooming house, and I've promised a Christmas Eve celebration that will make them think they're back home in Kiev."

Catherine had turned from him with a little contemptuous sniff. He caught her by the shoulder and shook her gently.

"Don't be so high-hat, young lady. Who knows, perhaps one of them might make a good husband!"

"Yes—a greenhorn from the old country—a *nice* husband!" she had flung back at him.

But anyway, the question of this year's Christmas had been settled, and Katrusia took a week off from the shop in order to clean the apartment and wash all the clothing and bedding. They didn't really need her at the shop, for work was slack. Olga couldn't help her—they were taking inventory at her place—and Catherine always had some excuse for not soiling her pretty hands. But all of them stayed at home on January sixth, working hard to have everything in readiness by the time the first star should appear in the sky.

It was still early when the girls came in with the bundles of hay and wheat, and broke in on Katrusia's reverie. She watched them arrange the wheat in a corner of the dining room, tuck some of the straw under the edge of the tablecloth, and throw the rest on the floor under the table.

"There!" exclaimed Catherine. "For the last time we throw all this litter about."

Katrusia smiled at her rebellious young daughter. "Perhaps—sometime—you understand," she said, fastening her best embroidered apron around her waist. She patted lovingly the broad border of black and red cross-stitch, and wondered if making

buttonholes in the tailor shop had spoiled her hands and her eyes for embroidering as she used to do. She left the girls to put the finishing touches to the table and went into the kitchen to be sure the fish in the oven was not getting too brown. She gave the borscht a swift stirring, set the pan of savory cabbage leaves stuffed with rice on the back of the stove, and wished aloud that Peter would come soon with his two guests, for the dinner was ready, and she was very hungry. The long days of fasting that preceded Christmas had been hard to observe this year; she must be growing old, she thought wistfully.

Yet she could still dance the *Hopak* and whirl and stamp as her daughters had never been able to do, and when she stood in her usual place in the very center of the Ukrainian chorus, arrayed in her beautiful costume, with the wreath of gay flowers and ribbons encircling her head, she knew she looked as young and pretty as any of the younger group.

Dusk had begun to gather in the streets, where already the snow had been trampled into mud and slush, when Peter came noisily into the room with his two guests.

Introductions over, they sat down at once at the loaded table, and Katrusia took the first spoonful from the traditional dish of wheat, from which each one must take a liberal mouthful before the remainder of the meal could be eaten.

"By the way, Mamusia," Peter swallowed the hot food hastily, "there are three old fellows over at the boardinghouse who are coming in to sing for us. They used to sing in the old country on

Christmas Eve. They can't find work, and one of them has been in prison for years and lost all his folks. They don't know English and haven't been here long. I hope they'll find the house. I wrote it all out for them to show somebody on the street—'*Vincent*, 185 First Street.'"

Katrusia rose suddenly to hide the tears that welled up into her eyes. How like Peter to invite the poor old men! But he couldn't guess what it would mean to his mother to have them sing. Perhaps it would be, "Yuletide wakes, Yuletide breaks."

"It's just what we need to make the evening perfect, Peter," she said. "I'll save enough of everything, so they can have plenty to eat for once."

Throughout the rest of the meal Katrusia sat at the head of the table, eating mechanically the food that she had so eagerly prepared. She heard as in a dream the gay talk and laughter of the young people. She stopped them when they threatened to throw to the ceiling a handful of *kutya*—the pudding made of wheat, honey, and poppy seed—which in the old country would bring good luck to all of them could they but make it stick up there. She was conscious of Catherine's kindling eyes as one of the young men talked, and was reminded once more of that Christmas so long ago when she had first seen Vanka. She realized dimly that the talk turned to more sober subjects and that scornful Catherine was duly impressed when their guests spoke enthusiastically of the Ukrainian poet Shevchenko, and admired his picture hanging on the wall. But all the time she was back in a

little village in Russia, and a young Cossack on a wild horse was riding toward her across the snowy plain.

They she heard the tramp of feet coming up the stairs, and her eyes glowed as she rose from her chair when Peter threw open the door.

But she sank back with a little sigh. Just three ragged old men, who must be listened to politely, fed, and sent away. They came close to the table and began to sing:

Yuletide wakes, Yuletide breaks,
Woman, give me eggs and cakes.

Once more Katrusia rose to her feet, her hand pressed hard against her beating heart. The man nearest her, the one who was most ragged and forlorn, stepped closer to her, and the song died in his throat.

"Vanka!" she cried.

"Katrusia?" It was a question and a sob.

Then all was confusion and excitement, explanations and tears.

It was Peter who fed the two other old men and sent them away; it was Catherine who asked Peter's young friends to go with them to church. Katrusia sat on in the quiet room with Vanka's hand in hers and thanked God for bringing him home on Christmas Eve.

Outside, the roofs and windowsills were white with snow, and church bells were ringing for midnight Mass.

What Amelia Wanted

Elsie Singmaster

Everything God does is right—the trademark on all his works is love.

PSALM 145:17, *THE MESSAGE*

This shall go here and that there." The widow Herr stood in the middle of the kitchen, her arms akimbo, her keen eyes surveying the collection of foodstuffs assembled on chairs and table and sink. She was large and stout; her dress was a beautiful, oft-washed gray gingham, draped across the shoulders with a little shawl of the same material. Though it was past the middle of the night, when full garb could scarcely be required of even the straitest of sects, she wore on her smooth hair the thin white cap which signified her full membership in the Church of the Brethren, called Dunkers by the world.

At this moment she frowned. She was not disturbed by finding herself thus surrounded at three o'clock in the morning, nor was she bewildered by the quantity of merchandise; she was merely directing her daughter, Amelia, how to pack the baskets and hampers which stood ready on the floor.

Amelia, too, wore a dress of oft-washed gingham, but the color was pale blue, and cap and shawl were lacking. She was still worldly; she had not yet been immersed or received into the church. Conscientious as Mrs. Herr was about religious matters, she had never insisted that Amelia become "plain"; eventually,

she was certain, Amelia would don the quiet garb. Amelia had a delicate complexion, but she was always well; she shuddered when her mother said that she herself had once been slender. She did not wish to grow broad and wear a Dunker cap. She was in love, and the object of her affection was of the world.

The vegetables and preserves and fowls and baked stuff were not the accumulation of months, but merely the merchandise carried by Mrs. Herr each Wednesday morning and Saturday afternoon to market at Harrisburg. On the table were pies and *Schwenkfelder* cakes and iced cakes and potato rolls and a huge platter of doughnuts. A turkey, a half-dozen chickens, and as many squabs lay side by side, their legs neatly crossed. In a row stood bowls of endive and celery, a crock of sauerkraut, and a crock of baked beans. The mantel was laden with jellies and preserves, flanked by glasses of walnut and hickory kernels and grated horseradish.

Mrs. Herr thought that Amelia didn't seem interested, but that did not prevent her from going on with her planning. She indicated the endive and celery with a sweep of her arm.

"These here, they go in the little basket. The baked stuff, except the *Fastnacht* cakes and the *Schwenkfelders,* shall go in one flat, the pies and layer cakes in the other. The buttermilk and cider you can carry at once to the wagon. I never held with those that pack overnight—things catch smells so. Mary Jonathan Herr, she had no sense; she once packed her onions with her other things overnight. It spoiled her trade. The *Schmierkäse* can go as it is, in the pitcher. The cup cheese you wrap nice up. Don't you feel good, Amelia?"

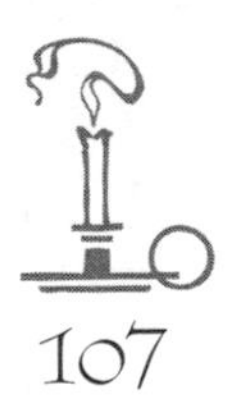

Amelia said absently, “Of course I feel good!” She took her shawl from the peg behind the door and wrapped it round her. Outside, the deaf and dumb hired man grunted to the white mare, which never set one foot before the other unless she was urged. He flung the door open and he and Amelia began to carry out the commodities and place them in the small covered wagon.

Amelia moved as though treading on air. Already in her imagination she was seated beside the deaf and dumb man, her folded arms hugging her pleasant thoughts. She would see the dim glow of the city lights in the distance, then the broad gray ribbon of the Susquehanna; she would watch the lights pale, and the east turn from gray to pink and blue and green and gold as the sun rose. It was only lately that she had been thrilled by the glories of the sunrise.

The drive to market was the happiest time of her life. Even the few minutes which the strange young man spent before her stall were not so blissful, because in his presence she scarcely dared look up. He was not so tall as to be alarming and he had curly hair and bright, brown eyes. When he left, her eyes followed him down the aisle to the corner of the market house where a young city woman sold goods from a bakery. She was tall and self-possessed, and she dressed with shocking bareness of neck and arm. Amelia did not like to look at her but she could not keep her eyes away. The city girl laughed loudly at what the young man said, and once, leaning over the counter, she gave him a playful push. Amelia hated her.

The sky was bright with stars; otherwise the world was dark,

except for the light which shone from the kitchen door and the reflection in the little stream flowing a few yards from the house. The whitewashed fence showed straight and ghostly; the ovals of clam shells surrounding flower beds, whose plants now flourished in windows, were vaguely discernible. Amelia sniffed a leafy odor from the woods nearby. It was almost the middle of December, but there had been little frost and a good deal of rain and the woods smelled like summer. Mrs. Herr continued to supervise the carrying out of baskets. She directed the hired man with signs and her daughter with words. "The pies shall be fifteen cents, Amelia, unless they don't go so quick, then ten." She paused for a response but received none. "If you can't sell the last chicken quick, then bring it home. It might be someone would come tomorrow account of Deardorf's funeral. Do you hear, Amelia?"

"Yes, Mom."

"And bring thread home, white thread, two dozen spools, so I can get at the quilting. And buy you a pair of shoes. Are you tired, Amelia?" Without answering, Amelia climbed into the wagon. "One of these days I go once more to market. It's hard for you. I'm stronger. I—"

If Mrs. Herr finished her sentence, her daughter did not hear. The deaf and dumb man lifted the reins, the wagon moved. Amelia clasped her hands.

"I must go to market," she said, aloud. "Whatever happens, I must go."

Until the wagon turned from the muddy lane into Route Fifteen, which crossed the many states, they had no companions.

Then they met rumbling trucks piled with bootlegged coal, and were overtaken by huge oil tanks whose drivers wished the little wagon off the face of the earth. The river showed gray between its lighted banks, the dome of the Capitol gleamed like a stupendous pearl.

They descended a hill and were on a long bridge, cars accumulating behind them. Amelia began to grow nervous, even though the young man never came to the stall before eight, when he stopped on his way to work, and it was not yet six. She nudged the hired man and leaned forward, imitating a hand lashing the mare's back. The hired man grunted, but he did not hurry the mare.

The Herr stall in the market house on the hill was small and obscure, but the Herr baskets always returned empty. Mrs. Herr's customers would have no other butter, no other eggs, no other dressed fowls. As Amelia was one of the first to arrive, she had hitherto been almost the first to leave, but lately she had lingered, keeping a few articles under the counter. When the young man did not come at eight, he came at twelve. He bought no staple food such as a householder would buy, but cakes and pies for a bachelor's lunch. He walked swiftly; Amelia could always see him far up the long aisle. She would catch her breath and close her eyes and lo! there he would be, laughing at her.

"Well!" he would say, "how's the pie crop this morning?" Or, "How about the cruller tree?"

Occasionally he ate a small pie or a doughnut or cruller as he stood before the stall. He always stopped to talk to the hateful

girl at the corner before he passed out the main door. Amelia believed the girl hailed him in a free way and asked him to stop. Amelia did not know his name or where he lived or what his work was; she blushed at a wish that the hired man were not deaf and dumb, so that she might ask him to follow the young man.

The arched market house had never appeared so beautiful. Christmas wreaths hung before many stalls as samples from which the country people would take orders. A florist had rented a stall and Amelia looked past masses of feathery fern fronds. Finding a fern on the sawdust-covered floor, she brushed it off and pinned it to her dress. She sniffed the odor of roses and carnations and her cheeks glowed.

The eggs were gone in fifteen minutes, all the vegetables in a half hour. It was six o'clock, then seven, then half past; it was eight and eight-fifteen, and still the young man had not come. Amelia sighed; then she smiled; then she frowned. It was pleasanter to have the young man's visit in the future than in the past. But her counter was almost empty—her neighbors would wonder why she lingered.

When only one *Schwenkfelder* cake remained, she told what was almost a lie.

"I'll take that," said a customer, opening the lid of her basket. "Ach, it's already taken!" said Amelia, quick as a flash. She flushed crimson. It was not quite a lie—the cake belonged to the young man who always bought something. The young man did not come; instead, the deaf and dumb man inquired with

uncouth gestures why she did not leave. He hung the baskets and pails on his arm and stacked the crocks.

The girl at the baker's stall had given her baskets to the baker's man, and she was now patting into place the curls which hung on her neck. Unconsciously Amelia patted her own hair, which waved from the root and not merely at the tips. If only the baker's clerk would go quickly! Perhaps the young man might still come. Tears filled Amelia's eyes—she could postpone departure no longer. Her hand shook as she lifted the *Schwenkfelder* cake.

As she put her foot on the step of the wagon, she glanced across the street. The baker's clerk stood at the corner waiting for a bus. No, she was not waiting for a bus; she was waiting for the young man who came hurrying up the street.

Amelia's foot, with the weight of her body already upon it, slipped, and she struck her knee against the sharp edge of the iron step. With guttural expressions of sympathy and alarm, the deaf and dumb man lifted her to the seat. She forgot the *Schwenkfelder* cake rolling on the ground, she forgot the thread for her mother's quilting, she forgot her new shoes, she hid her face and wept.

When she reached the farm her mother helped her into the house. Mrs. Herr made signs to the hired man, and he drove the wagon rapidly toward Route Fifteen and the doctor's. He was afraid that Amelia might die.

Amelia's injury proved to be a bruised and torn ligament; the doctor forbade her to take a step till he came again.

"But I'll have to go Saturday afternoon to market!"

"What foolish talk!" cried Mrs. Herr. "I go Saturdays. Why would you limp to market, Amelia? You have a mother." Mrs. Herr had a militant air, as though she meant to do battle for Amelia. Amelia wanted something, and so far she had always got for Amelia what she wanted.

On Saturday afternoon Amelia had her cheek against the back of the rocking chair. Her leg was elevated on another chair; beside her on the table was sewing and an abundant supper covered by lids and napkins. She said to herself that whatever happened she would go to market on Wednesday. She saw the bright-eyed young man stepping down the aisle, his eyes seeking her, then finding her mother. Her mother would be laughing and talking with the men and women in the stalls on either side; she would pay no attention to the young man. Worse still, the young man would pay no attention to her, except, perhaps, to be a little amused. He would turn at once to the baker's clerk.

On Wednesday Amelia could not stir. Her mother helped her dress and Amelia watched her pack the baskets and drive away with the hired man into the darkness. She begged her to wear her black dress, instead of the stiffly starched gray gingham, and her mother stared at her amazed.

"Shall I drag my Sunday dress in the sawdust, or get grease on it, or something sticky, say?"

Early in the afternoon, Mrs. Herr was at home.

"I sold by ten o'clock out," she boasted. "I can sell faster than

you, Amelia. Then I went in the store. I got the thread and the new shoes and a dress yet for you. See!"

Amelia's heart could not repress a throb of joy. The material was Alice-blue wool, the color of her eyes, her color. But for whom should she wear it?

"All bought wreaths and bunches of holly. It's a waste to make so much of Christmas. We don't make so much in our religion. Pretty near everything people buy gets afterwards thrown out. A chicken I like to have always, or a guinea, but that's not wasteful—you have to eat, if it is Christmas."

"Did you have many—many new customers?"

"No, not to say many. My old customers snapped everything too quick up. They were glad to see me. Next week, while you're still sitting, you can sew your dress."

Amelia's sad thoughts traveled to Saturday. By that time the young man would hardly cast a glance toward her corner. Doubtless, if he came to market, he would escort the baker's clerk to her home. Perhaps he would go with her to church on Sunday. Amelia saw herself sitting in Dunker meeting with the wonderful stranger across the aisle on the men's side. People had odd ways in worldly churches—it was said men and women sat together.

"Don't you like your new dress?" asked Mrs. Herr.

"Ach, to be sure!"

On Saturday Amelia was still unable to walk. Her cheeks were pale, her eyes dull, her dress only begun. The doctor came to call,

pronounced the knee better, forbade her to walk for another week, ate two doughnuts and drank a glass of cider, and went away.

On Wednesday Mrs. Herr spent only a few hours at market. Together with her empty baskets she brought news—at which Amelia's cheeks paled.

"That one at the corner, Amelia, did you see her?"

"Yes, I did."

"Well, I don't like that one. She's too—too bare, and too English for me. It's a nice young man talks to her. He's too good for that one."

"He is. Oh, he is!" echoed Amelia's soul.

By Saturday the color had still not returned to Amelia's cheeks. She could not sleep till late at night and she woke each morning with a start which made her whole body ache. She determined not to think of the young man, but her resolutions were vain. At noon she was still in bed. She could hobble without help from the sitting room, where she slept, into the kitchen. There was no place for her in the kitchen until the enormous assemblage of Christmas cakes and pies was removed.

"I don't like to go, and you alone," said Mrs. Herr, uneasily.

"Of course go!" Amelia thought she had never seen her mother look so large and so plain. She cried when the wagon drove away. The ground was frozen hard now and the wheels creaked. She followed it in her thoughts along the road, to the concrete highway, across the bridge. She saw the bright market house. People would shout "Merry Christmas!"—it was lovely to hear them.

There would be wreaths and festoons everywhere and every single article would be swept from the counters by excited buyers. She rose and dressed and hobbled into the kitchen.

Mrs. Herr did not return till late in the evening, and Amelia was still up. Her cheeks burned feverishly; she expected news of the hateful young woman. All afternoon she had sat with her sewing in her lap, but she did not even complete the hem already half-done.

"Something might happen," she said to herself. "No, nothing will happen. What could happen?"

Mrs. Herr bustled into the kitchen; the deaf and dumb man came grunting behind. He clapped his hands as a sign of satisfaction with Amelia's improvement. Mrs. Herr sat down and took off her bonnet and let her shawl drop from her shoulders.

"You look right good, Amelia."

Amelia tried to smile.

"I sold everything, but again I was talking."

Amelia had suddenly a recurrence of a sickening fear. Her mother's cheeks were red, her eyes danced; more than one Dunker widower had courted her.

"Why, your dress is almost finished!" cried Mrs. Herr.

"At last."

Mrs. Herr held up the dress and gazed at it admiringly. The disapproval of the elders would be strong indeed—Amelia had cut the neck in a V.

"Are you very tired, Amelia?"

"Not so very." Amelia leaned back her head.

"I talked to a young man from Ohio," said Mrs. Herr.

"From Ohio?" There was a close connection between the Dunkers in Pennsylvania and those in Ohio—perhaps her mother had taken a fancy to a young Dunker. "Does he visit the meetings?"

"No," answered Mrs. Herr. "This is the way. A week ago, he came to buy a *Schwenkfelder* or other baked things, and my baked things were all gone. It spited me, he was such a nice young man. Then he went and bought such baker's crullers from that girl—I told you about her. Baker's crullers are poison. So is she poison. He was such a nice young man, I walked in one piece after him to the door. I said to him, 'Do you always come to market?' 'Yes,' he said, he did. 'Well,' I said, 'you come Wednesdays and I have a *Schwenkfelder* for you.' Well, Wednesday he was there." The eyes of Mrs. Herr sparkled; it was possible to understand how she had once looked like Amelia.

"He was!" breathed Amelia, not knowing that she had spoken.

"He was. He said it was queer, I was a new one at the stall, but the *Schwenkfelder* was the same. I said I was your mother, and he asked me three times in five minutes about you. I had to tell him everything. I got everything out of him—what his name is and where he works—he gets more than a hundred dollars a month—and where he boards. He has a poor place to eat; it's a wonder he lives."

"Did he talk again to her?" breathed Amelia.

"I kept him till she was long gone," said Mrs. Herr. "She looked in his direction, but I kept his back all the time turned. He helped the deaf and dumb one carry the baskets and he stood long at the wagon and talked."

"Did he come this evening?"

"He did. His people are Plain People like us, Amelia. He said he pretty near jumped for joy when he seen my cap. I said he should come out to dinner tomorrow. I said we didn't make so much of Christmas, but we would of course eat. I kept back a chicken and I have ham, of course, and all vegetables, green and canned, and the mince pies are quick made. I make apple pie, too, and a custard. It won't be like sometimes, but it will do. He said—" Mrs. Herr clapped her hands across her mouth to stifle her words.

"You mean he comes here to dinner?"

"He does. He comes in the bus to the corner; from there he walks."

"Tomorrow?"

"Tomorrow. December twenty-five. Twelve o'clock."

"What else did he say?"

"He said—" Mrs. Herr hung the blue dress carefully over the back of a chair. She began to laugh and her laughter filled the kitchen and the house. "He said I look beautiful to him."

"He did?" Amelia looked at her mother and again tears came into her eyes. "You look beautiful to me, Mom," she said.

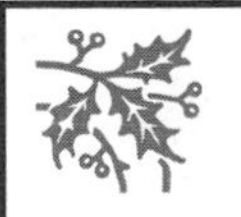

To Springvale for Christmas

Zona Gale

"Truly I tell you, this poor widow has put in more than all of them; for they all contributed out of their abundance, but she out or her poverty put in all the living that she had."

Luke 21:3-4, RSV

When President Arthur Tilton of Briarcliff College, who usually used a two-cent stamp, said, “Get me Chicago, please,” his secretary was impressed, looked for vast educational problems to be in the making, and heard instead:

“Ed? Well, Ed, you and Rick and Grace and I are going out to Springvale for Christmas.... Yes, well, I’ve got a family too, you recall. But mother was seventy last fall and—Do you realize that it’s eleven years since we all spent Christmas with her? Grace has been every year. She’s going this year. And so are we! And take her the best Christmas she ever had, too. Ed, mother was *seventy* last fall—”

At dinner, he asked his wife what would be a suitable gift, a very special gift, for a woman of seventy. And she said: “Oh, your mother. Well, dear, I should think the material for a good wool dress would be right. I’ll select it for you, if you like—” He said that he would see, and he did not reopen the subject.

In town on December twenty-fourth he timed his arrival to allow him an hour in a shop. There he bought a silver-gray silk of a fineness and lightness which pleased him and at a price which

made him comfortably guilty. And at the shop, Ed, who was Edward McKillop Tilton, head of a law firm, picked him up.

"Where's your present?" Arthur demanded.

Edward drew a case from his pocket and showed him a tiny gold wristwatch of decent manufacture and explained: "I expect you'll think I'm a fool, but you know that mother has told time for fifty years by the kitchen clock, or the parlor clock that never works—you get the idea?—and so I bought her this."

At the station was Grace, and the boy who bore her bag bore also a parcel of great dimensions.

"Mother already had a feather bed," Arthur reminded her.

"They won't let you take an automobile into the coach," Edward warned her.

"It's a rug for the parlor," Grace told them. "You know it *is* a parlor—one of the few left in the Mississippi Valley. And mother has had that ingrain down since before we left home—"

Grace's eyes were misted. Why would women always do that? This was no occasion for sentiment. This was a merry Christmas.

"Very nice. And Ricky'd better look sharp," said Edward dryly.

Ricky never did look sharp. About trains he was conspicuously ignorant. He had no occupation. Some said that he "wrote," but no one had ever seen anything that he had written. He lived in town—no one knew how—never accepted a cent from his brothers and was beloved of everyone, most of all of his mother.

"Ricky won't bring anything, of course," they said.

But when the train pulled out without him, observably, a

porter came staggering through the cars carrying two great suitcases and following a perturbed man of forty-something who said, "Oh, here you are!" as if it were they who were missing, and squeezed himself and his suitcases among brothers and sister and rug. "I had only a minute to spare," he said regretfully. "If I'd had two, I could have snatched some flowers. I flung 'em my card and told 'em to send 'em."

"Why are you taking so many lugs?" they wanted to know.

Ricky focused on the suitcases. "Just necessities," he said. "Just the presents. I didn't have room to get in anything else."

"Presents! What?"

"Well," said Ricky, "I'm taking books. I know mother doesn't care much for books, but the bookstore's the only place I can get trusted."

They turned over his books: fiction, travels, biography, a new illustrated edition of the Bible—they were willing to admire his selection. And Grace said confusedly but appreciatively: "You know, the parlor bookcase has never had a thing in it excepting a green curtain over it."

And they were all borne forward, well-pleased.

Springvale has eight hundred inhabitants. As they drove through the principal street at six o'clock on that evening of December twenty-fourth, all that they expected to see abroad was the popcorn wagon and a cat or two. Instead they counted seven automobiles and estimated thirty souls, and no one paid the slightest attention to them as strangers. Springvale was becoming metro-

politan. There was a new church on one corner and a store building bore the sign "Public Library." Even the little hotel had a rubber plant in the window and a strip of cretonne overhead.

The three men believed themselves to be a surprise. But, mindful of the panic to be occasioned by four appetites precipitated into a Springvale ménage, Grace had told. Therefore the parlor was lighted and heated, there was in the air of the passage an odor of brown gravy which, no butler's pantry ever having inhibited, seemed a permanent savory. By the happiest chance, Mrs. Tilton had not heard their arrival nor—the parlor angel being in her customary eclipse and the kitchen grandfather's clock wrong—had she begun to look for them. They slipped in, they followed Grace down the hall, they entered upon her in her gray gingham apron worn over her best blue serge, and they saw her first in profile, frosting a lemon pie. With some assistance from her, they all took her in their arms at once.

"Aren't you surprised?" cried Edward in amazement.

"I haven't got over being surprised," she said placidly, "since I first heard you were coming!"

She gazed at them tenderly, with flour on her chin, and then said: "There's something you won't like. We're going to have the Christmas dinner tonight."

Their clamor that they would entirely like that did not change her look.

"Our church couldn't pay the minister this winter," she said, "on account of the new church building. So the minister and his

wife are boarding around with the congregation. Tomorrow's their day to come here for a week. It's a hard life and I didn't have the heart to change 'em."

Her family covered their regret as best they could and entered upon her little feast. At the head of her table, with her four "children" about her, and father's armchair left vacant, they perceived that she was not quite the figure they had been thinking her. In this interval they had grown to think of her as a pathetic figure. Not because their father had died, not because she insisted on Springvale as a residence, not because of her eyes. Just pathetic. Mothers of grown children, they might have given themselves the suggestion, were always pathetic. But here was mother, a definite person, with poise and with ideas, who might be proud of her offspring, but who, in her heart, never forgot that they *were* her offspring and that she was the parent stock.

"I wouldn't eat two pieces of that pie," she said to President Tilton; "it's pretty rich." And he answered humbly, "Very well, mother."

And she took with composure Ricky's light chant:

"Now, you must remember, wherever you are,
That you are the jam, but your mother's the jar."

"Certainly, my children," she said. "And I'm about to tell you when you may have your Christmas presents. Not tonight. Christmas Eve is no proper time for presents. It's stealing a day

outright! And you miss the fun of looking forward all night long. The only proper time for the presents is after breakfast on Christmas morning, *after* the dishes are washed. The minister and his wife may get here any time from nine on. That means we've got to get to bed early!"

President Arthur Tilton lay in his bed looking at the muslin curtain on which the street lamp threw the shadow of a bare elm which he remembered. He thought: "She's a pioneer spirit. She's the kind who used to go ahead anyway, even if they had missed the emigrant party, and who used to cross the plains alone. She's the backbone of the world. I wish I could megaphone that to the students at Briarcliff who think their mothers 'try to boss' them!"

"Don't leave your windows open too far," he heard from the hall. "The wind's changed."

In the light of a snowy morning the home parlor showed the cluttered commonplace of a room whose furniture and ornaments were not believed to be beautiful and most of them known not to be useful. Yet when—after the dishes were washed—these five came to the leather chair which bore the gifts, the moment was intensely satisfactory. This in spite of the sense of haste with which the parcels were attacked—lest the minister and his wife arrive in their midst.

"That's one reason," Mrs. Tilton said, "why I want to leave part of my Christmas for you until I take you to the train tonight. Do you care?"

"I'll leave a present I know about until then too," said Ricky. "May I?"

"Come on now, though," said President Arthur Tilton. "I want to see mother get her dolls."

It was well that they were not of an age to look for exclamations of delight from mother. To every gift her reaction was one of startled rebuke.

"Grace, how could you? All that money! Oh, it's beautiful! But the old one would have done me all my life.... Why, Edward! You extravagant boy! I never had a watch in my life. You ought not to have gone to all that expense. Arthur Tilton! A silk dress! What a firm piece of goods! I don't know what to say to you—you're all too good to me!"

At Ricky's books she stared and said: "My dear boy, you've been very reckless. Here are more books than I can ever read—now. Why, that's almost more than they've got to start the new library with. And you spent all that money on me!"

It dampened their complacence, but they understood her concealed delight and they forgave her an honest regret of their modest prodigality. For, when they opened her gifts for them, they felt the same reluctance to take the hours and hours of patient knitting for which these stood.

"Hush, and hurry," was her comment, "or the minister'll get us!"

The minister and his wife, however, were late. The second side of the turkey was ready and the mince pie hot when, toward

noon, they came to the door—a faint little woman and a thin man with beautiful, exhausted eyes. They were both in some light glow of excitement and disregarded Mrs. Tilton's efforts to take their coats.

"No," said the minister's wife. "No. We do beg your pardon. But we find we have to go into the country this morning."

"It is absolutely necessary that we go into the country," said the minister earnestly. "This morning," he added impressively.

"Into the country! You're going to be here for dinner."

They were firm. They had to go into the country. They shook hands almost tenderly with these four guests. "We just heard about you in the post office," they said. "Merry Christmas—oh, Merry Christmas! We'll be back about dark."

They left their two shabby suitcases on the hall floor and went away.

"All the clothes they've got between them would hardly fill these up," said Mrs. Tilton mournfully. "Why on earth do you suppose they'd turn their back on a dinner that smells so good and go off into the country at noon on Christmas Day? They wouldn't do that for another invitation. Likely somebody's sick," she ended, her puzzled look denying her tone of finality.

"Well, thank the Lord for the call to the country," said Ricky shamelessly. "It saved our day."

They had their Christmas dinner; they had their afternoon—safe and happy and uninterrupted. Five commonplace-looking folk in a commonplace-looking house, but the eye of love knew

that this was not all. In the wide sea of their routine they had found and taken for their own this island day, unforgettable.

"I thought it was going to be a happy day," said Ricky at its close, "but it hasn't. It's been heavenly! Mother, shall we give them the rest of their presents now, you and I?"

"Not yet," she told them. "Ricky, I want to whisper to you."

She looked so guilty that they all laughed at her. Ricky was laughing when he came back from that brief privacy. He was still laughing mysteriously when his mother turned from a telephone call.

"What do you think?" she cried. "That was the woman that brought me my turkey. She knew the minister and his wife were to be with me today. She wants to know why they've been eating at a lunch counter out that way. Do you suppose—"

They all looked at one another doubtfully, then in abrupt conviction. "They went because they wanted us to have the day to ourselves!"

"Arthur," said Mrs. Tilton with immense determination, "let me whisper to you, too." And from that moment's privacy he also returned smiling, but a bit ruefully.

"Mother ought to be the president of a university," he said.

"Mother ought to be the head of a law firm," said Edward.

"Mother ought to write a book about herself," said Ricky.

"Mother's mother," said Grace, "and that's enough. But you're all so mysterious, except me."

"Grace," said Mrs. Tilton, "you remind me that I want to whisper to you."

Their train left in the late afternoon. Through the white streets they walked to the station, the somber little woman, the buoyant, capable daughter, the three big sons. She drew them to seclusion down by the baggage room and gave them four envelopes.

"Here's the rest of my Christmas for you," she said. "I'd rather you'd open it on the train. Now, Ricky, what's yours?"

She was firm to their protests. The train was whistling when Ricky owned up that the rest of his Christmas present for his mother was a brand-new daughter, to be acquired as soon as his new book was off the press. "We're going to marry on the advance royalty," he said importantly, "and live on—" The rest was lost in the roar of the express.

"Edward!" shouted Mrs. Tilton. "Come here. I want to whisper—"

She was obliged to shout it, whatever it was. But Edward heard, and nodded, and kissed her. There was time for her to slip something in Ricky's pocket and for the other goodbyes, and then the train drew out. From the other platform they saw her brave, calm face against the background of the little town. A mother of "grown children" pathetic? She seemed to them at that moment the one supremely triumphant figure in life.

They opened their envelopes soberly and sat soberly over the contents. The note, scribbled to Grace, explained: Mother wanted to divide up now what she had had for them in her will. She would keep one house and live on the rent from the other one, and "here's all the rest." They laughed at her postscript:

"Don't argue. I ought to give the most—I'm the mother."

"And look at her," said Edward solemnly. "As soon as she heard about Ricky, there at the station, she whispered to me that she wanted to send Ricky's sweetheart the watch I'd just given her. Took it off her wrist then and there."

"That must be what she slipped in my pocket," said Ricky. It was.

"She asked me," he said, "if I minded if she gave those books to the new Springvale Public Library."

"She asked me," said Grace, "if I cared if she gave the new rug to the new church that can't pay its minister."

President Arthur Tilton shouted with laughter.

"When we heard where the minister and his wife ate their Christmas dinner," he said, "she whispered to ask me whether she might give the silk dress to her when they get back tonight."

All this they knew by the time the train reached the crossing where they could look back on Springvale. On the slope of the hill lay the little cemetery, and Ricky said:

"And she told me that if my flowers got there before dark, she'd take them up to the cemetery for Christmas for father. By night she won't have even a flower left to tell her we've been there."

"Not even the second side of the turkey," said Grace, "and yet I think—"

"So do I," her brothers said.

Christmas Eve on Lonesome

John Fox, Jr.

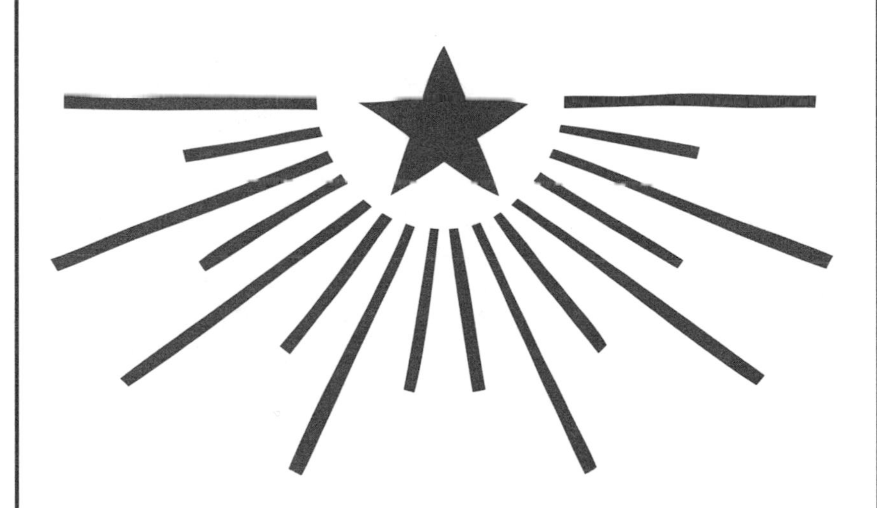

Beloved, never avenge yourselves,
but leave it to the wrath of God;
for it is written,
"Vengeance is mine,
I will repay, says the Lord."

ROMANS 12:19, RSV

It was Christmas Eve on Lonesome. But nobody on Lonesome knew that it was Christmas Eve, although a child of the outer world could have guessed it, even out in those wilds where Lonesome slipped from one lone log cabin high up the steeps, down through a stretch of jungled darkness to another lone cabin at the mouth of the stream.

There was the holy hush in the gray twilight that comes only on Christmas Eve. There were the big flakes of snow that fell as they never fall except on Christmas Eve. There was a snowy man on horseback in a big coat, and with saddle-pockets that might have been bursting with toys for children in the little cabin at the head of the stream.

But not even he knew that it was Christmas Eve. He was thinking of Christmas Eve, but it was of Christmas Eve of the year before, when he sat in prison with a hundred other men in stripes, and listened to the chaplain talk of peace and good-will to all men upon earth, when he had forgotten all men upon earth but one, and had only hatred in his heart for him.

"Vengeance is mine!" saith the Lord.

That was what the chaplain had thundered at him. And then, as now, he thought of the enemy who had betrayed him to the law, and had sworn away his liberty, and had robbed him of

everything in life except a fierce longing for the day when he could strike back and strike to kill. And then, while he looked back hard into the chaplain's eyes, and now, while he splashed through the yellow mud thinking of that Christmas Eve, Buck shook his head; and then, as now, his sullen heart answered, "Mine!"

The big flakes drifted to crotch and twig and limb. They gathered on the brim of Buck's slouch hat, filled out the wrinkles in his big coat, whitened his hair and his long mustache, and sifted into the yellow twisting path that guided his horse's feet.

High above he could see through the whirling snow now and then the gleam of a red star. He knew it was the light from his enemy's window; but somehow the chaplain's voice kept ringing in his ears, and every time he saw the light he couldn't help thinking of the story of the Star that the chaplain had told that Christmas Eve, and he dropped his eyes by and by, so as not to see it again, and rode on until the light shone in his face.

Then he led his horse up a little ravine and hitched it among the snowy holly and rhododendrons, and slipped toward the light. There was a dog somewhere, of course; and like a thief he climbed over the low rail fence and stole through the tall snow-wet grass until he leaned against an apple tree with the sill of the window two feet above the level of his eyes.

Reaching above him, he caught a stout limb and dragged himself up to a crotch of the tree. A mass of snow slipped softly to the earth. The branch creaked above the light wind; around the cor-

ner of the house a dog growled and he sat still.

He had waited three long years and he had ridden two hard nights and lain out two cold days in the woods for this.

And presently he reached out very carefully, and noiselessly broke leaf and branch and twig until a passage was cleared for his eye and for the point of the pistol that was gripped in his right hand.

A woman was just disappearing through the kitchen door, and he peered cautiously and saw nothing but darting shadows. From one corner a shadow loomed suddenly out in human shape. Buck saw the shadowed gesture of an arm, and he cocked his pistol. That shadow was his man, and in a moment he would be in a chair in the chimney-corner to smoke his pipe, maybe—his last pipe.

Buck smiled—pure hatred made him smile—but it was mean, a mean and sorry thing to shoot this man in the back, dog though he was; and now that the moment had come a wave of sickening shame ran through Buck. No one of his name had ever done that before; but this man and his people had, and with their own lips they had framed palliation for him. What was fair for one was fair for the other, they always said. A poor man couldn't fight money in the courts; and so they had shot from the brush, and that was why they were rich now and Buck was poor—why his enemy was safe at home, and he was out here, homeless, in the apple tree.

Buck thought of all this, but it was no use. The shadow slouched suddenly and disappeared; and Buck was glad. With a

gritting oath between his chattering teeth he pulled his pistol in and thrust one leg down to swing from the tree—he would meet him face to face next day and kill him like a man—and there he hung as rigid as though the cold had suddenly turned him, blood, bones, and marrow, into ice.

The door had opened, and full in the firelight stood the girl who he had heard was dead. He knew now how and why that word was sent him. And now she who had been his sweetheart stood before him—the wife of the man he meant to kill.

Her lips moved—he thought he could tell what she said: "Git up, Jim, git up!" Then she went back.

A flame flared up within him now that must have come straight from the devil's forge. Again the shadows played over the ceiling. His teeth grated as he cocked his pistol, and pointed it down the beam of light that shot into the heart of the apple tree, and waited.

The shadow of a head shot along the rafters and over the fireplace. It was a madman clutching the butt of the pistol now, and as his eye caught the glinting sight and his heart thumped, there stepped into the square of light of the window—a child!

It was a boy with yellow tumbled hair, and he had a puppy in his arms. In front of the fire the little fellow dropped the dog, and they began to play.

"Yap! yap! yap!"

Buck could hear the shrill barking of the fat little dog, and the joyous shrieks of the child as he made his playfellow chase his tail round and round or tumbled him head over heels on the floor. It

was the first child Buck had seen for three years; it was *his* child and *hers;* and, in the apple tree, Buck watched fixedly.

They were down on the floor now, rolling over and over together; and he watched them until the child grew tired and tuned his face to the fire and lay still—looking into it. Buck could see his eyes close presently, and then the puppy crept closer, put his head on his playmate's chest, and the two lay thus asleep.

And still Buck looked—his clasp loosening on his pistol and his lips loosening under his stiff mustache—and kept looking until the door opened again and the woman crossed the floor. A flood of light flashed suddenly on the snow, barely touching the snow-hung tips of the apple tree, and he saw her in the doorway—saw her look anxiously into the darkness—look and listen a long while.

Buck dropped noiselessly to the snow when she closed the door. He wondered what they would think when they saw his tracks in the snow next morning; and then he realized that they would be covered before morning.

As he started up the ravine where his horse was, he heard the clink of metal down the road and the splash of a horse's hoofs in the soft mud, and he sank down behind a holly bush.

Again the light from the cabin flashed out on the snow.

"That you, Jim?"

"Yep!"

And then the child's voice: "Has oo dot thum tandy?"

"Yep!"

The cheery answer rang out almost at Buck's ear, and Jim passed death waiting for him behind the bush which his left foot brushed, shaking the snow from the red berries down on the crouching figure beneath.

Once only—far down the dark jungled way, with the underlying streak of yellow that was leading him whither, God only knew—once only Buck looked back. There was the red light gleaming faintly through the moonlit flakes of snow. Once more he thought of the Star, and once more the chaplain's voice came back to him.

"Mine!" saith the Lord.

Just how, Buck could not see, with himself in the snow and *them* back there for life with her and the child, but some strange impulse made him bare his head.

"Yourn," said Buck grimly.

But nobody on Lonesome—not even Buck—knew that it was Christmas Eve.

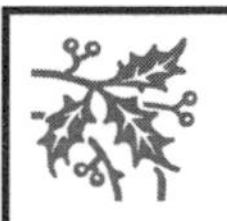

A Brand of His Own

Harry C. Rubicam, Jr.

. . . I caused the widow's heart
to sing for joy.

JOB 29:13, RSV

My host of the lonely campfire was unknown to me, but I saw at once that he was a prosperous cattleman. The firelight danced on a bronzed face hardened by that touch of arrogance which comes of exercising supreme authority over a vast domain. Yet he wore the air of complacency that sits on men who know their cattle are fat.

Since I had ridden out of the darkness into his circle of firelight, few words had passed between us beyond an exchange of greetings and his use of the traditional invitation to "light down and eat."

My horse was unsaddled and hobbled for the night, and I was spreading my canvas bedroll beside the fire, when he spoke suddenly:

"This is an awful way to spend Christmas Eve!"

I agreed, and we slipped easily into conversation, until finally I broached the subject that had been uppermost in my mind for hours.

"I saw a strange thing this afternoon," I told him. "In a stretch of prairie, miles from anywhere, I came upon a Franciscan friar putting flowers on a lonely grave. We waved to each other as I rode past but, curious as I was, I felt it was not a time to stop and

talk with him. I've wondered ever since about that grave, and why the padre was decorating it."

My host stared into the flames for a long moment.

"That was Padre Penado," he said finally. "He and I make a little ceremony of decorating that grave each Christmas Eve.

"He was to meet me there today, but he was late. I waited as long as I could; too long, in fact, that's why I'm benighted here. I'm glad to hear you say that the padre got there after all."

I knew better than to ask whose grave it was, or why it stood in need of decorating every Christmas Eve. And presently my silence was rewarded.

"There's a story about that grave," the cattleman began, "the story of a Christmas years ago, and of a man who understood the true spirit of Christmas."

And so he told me the story, and as nearly as I can remember, the way of it was this....

It seemed that Padre Penado had long since abandoned attempts at altering San Tobar's ideas as to how Christmas should be celebrated. He regretted that the prairie town persisted in marking Christ's nativity with the dusty violence of the saddling chute, but the good padre realized that, in spite of anything he could say, Christmas Day would remain Rodeo Day in San Tobar.

But this particular year, it seemed to the padre that even the rodeo radiated something of the Christmas spirit, for it grew increasingly apparent that the prize money was destined to do

much good in a worthy cause. And then word came of developments that filled the good padre with despair.

A Mission Indian came in with the report that Bill Cordova, former state bronco-busting champion, returning to the Circle Y Ranch after an absence of several years, planned to enter the riding contest, and would undoubtedly win. This seemed like a fatal blow to the padre's fondest hopes, for Cordova was as tough and hard-bitten an hombre as ever pounded leather, and was not a man whom the padre would ordinarily suspect of being steeped in the spirit of self-sacrifice.

But the Franciscan friar had never yet faltered in the face of what he conceived to be his duty, and so, the day before Christmas, Padre Penado found himself tooling his rattle-trap car along the two ruts that served as the road to the Circle Y.

Emerging from the large cloud of dust that marked the spot where he had brought his car to a creaking halt, the good padre saw Duke Andrews perched on the top pole of the horse corral, watching Bill Cordova saddle Hipockets, ace bucker of the Circle Y "mean string."

"Howdy, Padre!" Bill shouted. "Climb up beside the Duke an' see the fun!"

Padre Penado's long brown robe hindered him not at all as he easily swung his gaunt, muscular frame to the top of the high fence.

"Glad to see you back, my son," he said to Bill. "But aren't you a little old for this sort of thing?"

"A man's never too old to git throwed off a hoss!" Bill laughed, as he reached up to shake hands with the padre.

"Bill's goin' to ride in the Christmas rodeo," Duke Andrews announced.

"An' I'm goin' to win that championship again," Bill stated. "But I won't squander the five thousand dollars prize money like I done ten years ago. I aim to buy me a ranch, an' settle down, an' have stock an' a brand of my own!"

"You been standin' around in the sun without your hat," said old Albuquerque, veteran cowman and foreman of the Circle Y, as he sauntered up from the barn. "Why, hello, Padre; didn't see you.

"Look, Bill," he continued, "you're ten years older than you was that time you won the state championship. An' just because you can still ride old Hipockets is no sign you can top off the hosses they'll have at San Tobar."

"Most people seem to think young Kid Brewster will win this year," the padre said, innocently.

"I never seen this Kid ride, but I hear he's mighty good," Bill admitted, slapping down the stirrup with a loud pop of the fender. He swung easily into the saddle, and tested the hack reins for length. Then he leaned forward and was about to snatch the blindfold from the horse's head, when he paused.

"Any o' you gents got two silver dollars?" he demanded.

Albuquerque grinned as he produced two coins and walked toward the tensely-waiting horse. Hipockets, being blindfolded,

could be trusted not to stir a step, for a horse will not move when he cannot see where he's going. So Hipockets stood, steel muscles taut as catapult springs, waiting for the instant when the blindfold would be whisked away.

"Put a silver dollar in each stirrup, just under my boot," Bill directed.

When the coins were in place, Bill Cordova looked at Padre Penado.

"You know, Padre, the main thing in bronc ridin' is to keep your feet in them stirrups. That's what gives you the grip with your knees. If you lose either stirrup, the next move is to pick yourself up off the ground.

"Years gone by, we used to practice ridin' with dollars in the stirrups. Not many men can keep 'em there, but it learns you to keep your feet in the stirrups

"I ain't claimin' to ride like I used to could, but when this here hoss is through buckin', you'll find them dollars right where Albuquerque put 'em!"

This was the old trick for which Bill Cordova had once been famous, but Duke Andrews didn't believe he could still do it, and said so.

"If the padre wasn't here," he said, "I'd bet you some money on that!"

"Don't mind me!" the padre laughed. "I was thinking of placing a small bet myself!"

"I wouldn't take your money!" said Bill Cordova, as he leaned

forward and jerked the blindfold from Hipockets' head.

Old Hipockets, used to the business, stood stiff-legged for a second, then crouched as though drawing all his steel muscles together for one mighty effort, after which he launched into the jolting, wracking, bone-pounding, body-wrenching bucking that had made him top horse of the local buckers.

It was a full three minutes before the horse gave up, to stand dejectedly, with heaving sides and lowered head. Duke Andrews climbed down from the fence and examined Bill's stirrups, removing the silver dollars from beneath the rider's boots.

"Doggone!" he exclaimed. "I didn't think you could do it!"

"It's an old trick," Albuquerque told him, "but you got to be durned good to do it!"

"You bet!" the Duke agreed. "But look—doin' it on poor old Hipockets is one thing, an' doin' it on the man-killin' broncs they'll have at the state rodeo on Christmas Day is somethin' else!"

"You're right," Albuquerque admitted. "But I doubt if this Kid Brewster could do it on a rockin' hoss!"

"Some of the boys are having a practice session at the rodeo grounds this afternoon," Padre Penado said, as he climbed down off the fence. "Kid Brewster is going to ride."

"I'd like to see that," Bill Cordova stated.

"Hop in my car and I'll take you down," the padre offered. "I'd enjoy seeing it, too."

Old Albuquerque stared hard at the padre. The good father

was up to something, he reckoned, and being a shrewd operator, would bear watching. What was it to Padre Penado who won the contest? Why was he so anxious for Kid Brewster to win the prize money?

"Mind if I come along?" Albuquerque asked.

"Of course not!" said the padre, heartily. "Glad to have you!"

Padre Penado slipped behind the wheel, and Bill climbed in beside him while Albuquerque settled watchfully into the back seat. The thunderous roar of the old car's motor discouraged conversation, and few words were spoken until the padre turned briskly into the rodeo grounds at San Tobar.

Forty cowboys, dressed in colorful rodeo garb, were grouped around a high, narrow, saddling chute, the sides of which heaved and strained to the struggles of an imprisoned and infuriated horse. Two saddlers, working through the bars of the chute, adjusted a regulation "bear-trap" saddle on the bronco, while a sunburned, watchful-eyed youth stood nearby, hitching nervously at the belt of his wide leather chaps.

"That's Kid Brewster," Padre Penado volunteered.

Bill Cordova pressed closer to the chute, followed by Albuquerque, as Kid Brewster climbed the bars and eased himself into the saddle.

The chute gate swung wide and the horse lunged out, bawling with rage, pawing, kicking, rearing, and bucking viciously.

Bill watched with practiced eye as Kid Brewster sat his saddle, swaying lithely to the motions of the horse. A relieved sigh

escaped Cordova as he noted that the Kid, while a mighty good rider, did not sit with the ease and carelessness that should mark a championship contender. The Kid was good, very good, but not as good as Bill Cordova, and Bill knew it.

Albuquerque knew it, too, and mentioned the fact as the pick-up men galloped alongside the bucking horse and grabbed for the hack rein.

"If that's the best they've got to show," he muttered, "you're a cinch to win, Bill."

"I ain't underestimatin' the Kid none," Bill replied, modestly. "He's plenty good, but he's pretty young. In a couple years he'll mebby be ridin' circles around me, but right now I bet I can out-ride him."

As the pickup men halted the horse and helped the Kid to dis-mount, two cowhands began a loud discussion of the recent ride.

"He's sure good," said a tall, lank rider in a green shirt. "If he stayed around here another year or two, he'd be like to win more than just the state championship!"

"Yeah," his companion stated, "he's world championship stuff, that Kid. But why ain't he stayin' around here?"

"Aw, his Maw wants him to go to college!" said Green Shirt, in a tone of mild disgust.

"Why," said Bill Cordova, slipping easily into the conversation, cowboy fashion. "That's a break for the Kid. He's lucky his Maw can send him to college."

"But she can't!" Green Shirt replied. "She ain't got no money!"

"That's why the Kid is tryin' to win this five thousand dollars prize money on Christmas Day," one of the cowhands explained. "He aims to use the championship money for his eddication."

"I see." Bill Cordova spoke thoughtfully. "Then if the Kid don't win, he can't go to school?"

"That's right," the cowhand admitted. "An' that's why most folks around here is hopin' the Kid wins. Fact, is, he was a cinch to win hands down until we heard that some former champion name o' Bill Cordova had done up an' entered."

"Don't know him," said Green Shirt. "Must'a been before my time."

"Why, yeah," said a youth in a wide, black hat. "He was champion, take it here ten-twelve years ago. A real buckaroo, this Cordova, they tell me. But I still hope Kid Brewster wins."

"Mebby he will!" said Bill Cordova, turning on his high heel and striding away.

"Gee, he's a hard-lookin' guy!" said Green Shirt. "Who is he?"

"That," said old Albuquerque, spitting reflectively, "is Bill Cordova!"

"An' if I knows anythin' about Bill," he added, with a sour glance at the cowboys, "you chatterin' magpies done went an' put idees into his head!"

"What do you mean?" Padre Penado asked with an innocent air.

"You know what I mean!" Albuquerque growled. "That's what you brought Bill down here for! I knowed you was up to

somethin', out there at the ranch; that's why I come along, thinkin' to prevent it. But I reckon the harm's done now!"

A loud hail from Bill saved the padre the necessity of making a reply.

"Let's git a-goin'," Bill called and, as the friar and the old cowman joined him, he continued, "On the way home I'll show you the piece o' land I aim to buy with the prize money, Padre!"

Albuquerque stared hard at his old friend, and then grinned cheerfully. Reckon old Bill was goin' through with it, at that! Should'a knowed all this sob-stuff about the Kid's college education couldn't throw a tough old waddie like Bill off the track!

"Mind if I stop in town first?" Padre Penado asked. "It won't take but fifteen minutes or so."

"Sure not!" Bill agreed, as they climbed into the car.

The padre parked beside a wooden hitching rail, and leaped out, promising to return as soon as possible. Old Albuquerque slouched in the back seat, but Bill got out, saying he'd step down to the corner and buy tobacco.

As Bill stumped along the board sidewalk, a middle-aged woman, prematurely gnarled and bent with work, came struggling toward him carrying a large bag of laundry. As she reached the corner, there came a quick pounding of hoofs, and a dozen mounted cowboys whirled into sight, laughing, shouting and whooping.

The woman gave a startled scream, dropped her bundle on the ground, and darted into a doorway. The cowboys, unaware of the woman's fright, whirled away in a cloud of dust.

153

Bill Cordova hurried to the corner and picked up the laundry bag.

"Oh, them awful cowhands!" the woman cried, angrily. "I never see such goin's-on!"

"Why, ma'am, the boys don't mean no harm," Bill explained. "They're just in town for the rodeo. You let me tote this here bag a ways, ma'am, it's too heavy for you."

"I'll manage," she said, resolutely, seizing hold of the bundle. Then her glance took in Bill's hat, his boots, the lithe slimness of his tall figure.

"Well, I see you're a cowboy, too!" she said, in some confusion. "What I said about cowboys, I'm sure I didn't mean you!"

"That's all right, ma'am," Bill laughed. "Reckon we do seem kind o' rough to a lady. But bein' a cowboy ain't no gentleman's game."

"That's what I tell my son," the woman relied. "Can't understand why anyone wants to be a cowboy!"

"I judge you don't think much of us cow-waddies, ma'am!"

"Why should I?" she demanded, as they started along the street, Bill carrying the bundle which he had retained after a brief struggle.

"Look at me!" she continued. "I married a cowboy; that's why I has to take in washin'! Cowhands is mostly right nice people, but they just ain't no good!"

"Why, ma'am, we work awful hard!" Bill objected. "An' it's plumb useful work!"

"Sure you work hard, but where does it git you!" the woman demanded. "You ever seen a cowboy yet that had any money, or any decent clothes, or any chance of ever gittin' any?

"You work hard; don't tell me! Ten to sixteen hours a day in the saddle, come all kinds o' weather; mebby sleepin' on the ground at night, an' it wet, like as not; eatin' hard bread, burned beans an' black coffee, an' for what? For forty dollars a month, an' your keep, if you can call it that!

"No, sir! I want my boy to go to college, an' git the learnin' his Pa an' me never had. Then he won't have to work the way you work, eat the food you eat, wear the clothes you wear, never havin' a penny to his name except what prize money he can pick up riskin' his life at rodeos.

"My boy is goin' to college an' make somethin' of himself," she concluded, "or my name ain't Ma Brewster!"

"Oh, so you're Kid Brewster's mother!" Bill exclaimed.

"I am that! You know my boy?"

"No, ma'am, but I seen him ride just now, out to the rodeo grounds. He's good."

"Oh, he can ride, all right," the mother admitted, proudly. "So could his father before him, up until the time a horse fell on him an' killed him! I don't like for my boy to be ridin', an' I'm only lettin' him enter the Christmas rodeo because some folks think he can win. An' that five thousand dollars prize money would put him through college!"

There was a dreamy, far-away look in the woman's eyes as she continued:

"Five thousand dollars! A heap o' money! What a Christmas Day it would be for us, if he won. I could quit takin' in washin', an' move to Fort Collins, so'st to keep house for the Kid while he's in the Agricultural school, learnin' the things he'll need to help him git to be a big cattleman.

"But," she added, tonelessly, "reckon he'll not win. It'll prob'ly turn out like all my Christmases. I hear a former champion is comin' back to ride this year, an' folks says he's the best rider ever saddled a hoss."

They had reached the shack where Ma Brewster lived and worked; a single room, dank with the steamy odor of wash tubs and drying clothes. The homemade furniture, the broken-down bed with its feet buried in the dirt floor, the broken window stuffed with rags, spoke of an abject poverty such as even Bill Cordova had never known. Bill felt very uncomfortable as he set down the bundle of wash and Ma Brewster thanked him for carrying it.

"Suppose this former champion beats your boy?" Bill asked. "What will you do?"

"Why, I'll just go right on washin' other people's clothes for a livin'," Ma Brewster replied.

"He'll keep workin' for the Diamond D, I suppose. They're payin' him mighty little, that's why I has to take in washin', but it's the only job he can find."

"Mebby he'll win the money, ma'am," Bill said, "you can't tell; anything can happen in a ridin' contest. I'll be sayin' goodbye, now, ma'am."

156

It was a somewhat subdued Bill Cordova that found Albuquerque and Padre Penado waiting for him at the car. He volunteered no information as to where he had been and, Western fashion, they did not ask him.

It was just before sundown when the car rattled out of San Tobar along the road that led across the prairie. After half an hour of driving, Bill called a halt, and the three men climbed out into the sagebrush. Led by Bill, they walked up the slope of a ridge and when they reached the top, Bill pointed down into the flat land below.

It was a rolling prairie, brown with the curling buffalo grass, and in the foreground a tiny stream, lined with willows, wound and twisted.

"Right down there," Bill announced, "is where I aim to build my cabin!"

A jackrabbit hopped with limping stride between the soapweed clumps, and a lone antelope flashed a quick, white tail around a bend in the stream. Out in the sagebrush, a prairie dog barked, while in the willows a great horned owl boomed in a gloomy voice that set a flock of magpies to cursing horribly after the manner of their obscene kind. A meadowlark opened its black-chevroned throat and twanged a sweet, clear bugle call. Then all the birds were still as a distant coyote sent a long-drawn, quavering howl throbbing across the ridges.

"It is a beautiful piece of land," said Padre Penado, in a hushed voice.

"An' the prize money will buy it," Bill told him. "An' then I won't be Bill Cordova, no-account cowhand; I'll be W.C. Cordova, prominent rancher an' cattle-breeder!"

"And Kid Brewster will not go to college," said the padre.

"That's his look-out!" Albuquerque exploded, having stood all he was going to stand. "He's young, an' has lots o' time. Bill's gittin' old, an' this is his last chance to have what he's allus wanted! An' you're tryin' to git it away from him for the sake of some upstart kid!"

"Padre," said Bill, ignoring his friend's impassioned outburst, "I wanted to show you this spot so you'd understand why winnin' that prize money means so much to me.

"It's my last chance, Padre, to have what I want. Next year I'll be too old to ride in contests. I'm stretchin' a point to do it now. An' if I don't win that money, I'll just go on bein' a tramp, movin' from ranch to ranch, earnin' my keep an' a little tobacco money, until I'm too old to ride at all.

"Then I'll be just another poor old codger, hangin' around a town like San Tobar, sweepin' out stores for a meal now an' then. I've *got* to win that money; you understand that, Padre?"

"I understand," the padre nodded. "Kid Brewster is young, and may win another year. But, still, it is more blessed to give than to receive. And it is Christmas time, Bill."

"I got nothin' much to give," said Bill, "an' I never receive anything!"

"You have a great deal to give," the padre insisted. "But I

won't talk to you of the Christmas spirit."

"The Christmas spirit is the bunk!" Albuquerque snorted. "Looks to me like Christmas was invented to help storekeepers make a little extra money!"

"We used to have Christmas at home when I was a kid," Bill mused aloud. "My mother, she set a heap o' store by Christmas. But it don't mean nothin' to me no more!" he added, belligerently.

"We'll say no more about it," Padre Penado murmured. "Perhaps you need the money more than anyone else. You will have a fine ranch, and I'll be glad for that, at least."

They walked silently down the slope, and presently the car was jolting its way toward the Circle Y through the purple mist of a prairie twilight.

Bill Cordova lay awake for a long while that night, thinking, dreaming, struggling with this problem Padre Penado had presented him. Every time he closed his eyes, he saw the cabin he would build down there in the willows; saw the picturesque poles of the round corral he would build; saw himself standing in the doorway of the cabin, watching lines of white-faced cattle stringing down to the stream to drink. His cattle, bearing Bill Cordova's own brand! But, somehow, the bent figure of Ma Brewster kept crossing the foreground of his dreams, struggling bravely with large bundles of dirty clothes.

He began to think of his own mother; she had worked hard, too. He remembered the rough feel of her work-seamed hands,

the strained look of her gaunt, stoical face, the tired droop of her shoulders.

He remembered how, at Christmas time, her face had taken on a strange, glowing look as she rushed about, making candies, pies and cakes, cleaning house, hiding presents from prying young eyes, rigging decorations, and working herself happily to a point of exhaustion with the thousand and one chores that women of her day found necessary at Yuletide. She sure had set a heap of store by Christmas!

Yet Christmas had never been too elaborate at her house; she had frowned severely on the spending of too much money.

"'Tain't the size or the cost o' the gifts you give," she always said, "it's the spirit in which you give 'em that counts."

Christmas wasn't like that any more, Bill decided. People who had any money spent more than they could afford buying each other presents that none of them needed or really wanted, while to folks like Ma Brewster, Christmas was just a day when you didn't have to work quite as hard as usual. Wonder somebody wouldn't do something to help folks like the Brewsters.

Bill Cordova forced himself to stop thinking about it, realizing that he must get some sleep if he aimed to be in shape for the riding contest.

Christmas Day dawned bright and clear, warm enough for a man to ride in his shirt sleeves, yet with a sharp, clean tang to the dry air.

For miles in all directions the dust hung in the sky, dust whirled up by thousands of automobiles converging on San Tobar. By noon the stands at the rodeo grounds were jammed with spectators, and the arena was alive with bright-shirted cowboys, hard-faced cowgirls, and feather-decked Indians. And everywhere was dust.

Forlorn-looking pine trees, brought from the mountains by dint of much trouble, drooped dustily on the street corners, and evergreen boughs sagged over doorways. Here and there some aesthetic soul had contrived a Christmas wreath which hung, drying rapidly, in a window.

By mid-afternoon, everyone was at the rodeo grounds, and the events were being run off in rapid order. Many riders came hurtling out of the saddling chutes, and the featured bronco-busting contests narrowed to a few top hands, until finally all but Kid Brewster and Bill Cordova had been eliminated.

Excitement mounted as the Kid "put up a good ride, takin' mane an' tail at every jump," and for a moment, Padre Penado felt a quick upsurging of hope. Even Bill Cordova would be hard-pressed to win now.

"All right, folks," the announcer drawled. "Watch chute number two! Bill Cordova, former state champion, coming out of chute two on Noonday. Watch chute two, folks!"

Bill's ears were buzzing, and his hands trembled with the suppressed excitement, not unmixed with fear, that even the most experienced rider feels as he climbs the bars of the saddling chute.

He moved mechanically as he let himself down into the saddle and felt Noonday go taut beneath him.

"Here he comes, folks; Bill Cordova on Noonday!"

The band struck up a lively tune as Noonday lurched out of the chute, his great black back arched in a vicious plunge. Bill Cordova, wide chaps flopping, bright shirt billowing, clung like a leech to the saddle, his lithe figure swaying easily to the jolting, pounding motion of the frantic horse.

This was easy, Bill thought, as he caught the swing of the animal's antics and strained his muscles to meet the bronco's every move and trick.

Bill's ears hurt and his head swam, his eyes filled with tears and his nose began to bleed a little trickle that ran slowly down his chin as his punished body ached from the terrific jolting. He had never thrown a leg across a horse that was the equal of Noonday, but Bill was riding him, and he knew it.

The crowd knew it, too, and ten thousand people leaped to their feet in the roaring stands as the pickup men closed in to catch Noonday when his fight was over.

The horse was tiring rapidly now, and although he bucked and bawled and reared and snorted, his efforts were tame compared to his first tremendous antics, and Bill Cordova knew that in a few seconds more he would again be state champion bronco buster.

They couldn't tie this ride! Not Kid Brewster, nor nobody else! He was winning the prize money, and with it the thing he had always wanted, a ranch, and a brand of his own!

The Kid wouldn't get to go to college. Poor old Ma Brewster would sure be disappointed. But there was that piece of land, with a cabin right down in the willows.... Wouldn't be much of a Christmas for Ma and the Kid.

Guess they never had a real Christmas in their lives. Bill remembered Christmas at home when he was a boy, watching his father trim the tree. He had always had to go to bed before it was done, for he was told that Santa Claus would drop in and finish it during the night. He remembered the tinsel, the colored balls, and his mother's glowing excitement. What was it she had always said? Something about the spirit of Christmas.

"Aw, shucks!" said Bill Cordova, and his feet slipped out of the stirrups. The next instant the ground stopped revolving long enough to come sailing up and hit him a terrific, breath-destroying blow. The noise in the grandstand stopped abruptly, and Bill sat up in the dust, only to throw himself flat again as a pickup man's horse vaulted over him.

"Tough luck, cowboy!" said the pickup man. "You was doin' fine till you lost your stirrups!"

Bill stood up and slowly brushed the dust from his chaps and shirt. Then he carefully put on his hat, turned and walked from the arena, limping slightly.

"Well, that's that, folks!" bawled the loudspeaker. "Kid Brewster is now the state champion bronco buster!"

The crowd applauded boisterously as Kid Brewster, flushed and happy, rode to the judges' stand to receive the silver trophy

and the committee's check for five thousand dollars.

A lump rose in old Albuquerque's throat as he and Duke Andrews glanced at each other and then suddenly found something very interesting to stare at on the ground. They looked up at the sound of Padre Penado's sandals flapping in the dust.

"You saw!" said the padre, and the two cowmen nodded.

Then silence fell between them and each knew that the others were thinking of Bill, the man who could ride with silver dollars in his stirrups.

The lights of San Tobar twinkled and dwindled rapidly in the distance as Bill and his friends bumped along the dirt road in the ranch flivver.

"How come you lost your stirrups?" Albuquerque demanded, suddenly.

"Why," said Bill, "it just happened, I reckon. You know how it is."

"Yeah, we know how it is," Albuquerque replied, softly. "We seen you kick your feet loose!"

The cattleman sat motionless, staring into the fire. A quick gust of wind shouted along the prairie, and the bare cottonwoods moaned and chattered as something wet and cold fluttered against my face. I arose, knocked out my pipe, and crawled into my bedroll, while the cattleman buttoned his leather jacket against the softly falling snow.

"What happened to Bill Cordova?" I asked.

"He drifted out of this country. Went up into Montana, I think, for a few years. Finally he came back to the Circle Y, and was killed when a horse fell on him.

"The day Bill died, Padre Penado told me the story I've just told you. Until then only three men knew the truth, and they had kept their secret well, for Bill had made them promise that so long as he lived no one should know why he had lost his stirrups that Christmas Day.

"Well, I bought the piece of land Bill had always wanted, and we buried him right where he had planned to build his cabin."

"That was a fine thing for you to do!" I exclaimed.

"Oh, it was little enough," the cattleman replied. "You see, I was Kid Brewster."

"I Gotta Idee!"

Elsie Singmaster

A good wife who can find?
She is far more precious than jewels.

PROVERBS 31:10, RSV

Just before suppertime on Christmas Eve, Amelia Brodhead suffered a shock, the first of a series. She laid down her wooden spoon, covered her bread dough with a fragment of old tablecloth and a darned shawl, and stood the mixing bowl on a chair behind the stove. She was a short woman, thirty-five years old, with unnaturally large black eyes and the odd wrinkles of skin shrunk by a sudden falling away of flesh.

"Where are the children?" she asked impatiently.

Bill, the children's father, sat by the window staring at a steep hillside covered with snow. He, too, was small and thin; his large workman's hands, which were not brown and callused but white and soft, looked out of proportion to his body. He had long ago come from Pennsylvania to Colorado with other miners.

"Coasting," he said.

"They'll have the appetites of tigers," said Amelia. "It's their own fault if they go hungry to bed."

On the other side of the table Gran'ma Brodhead sat knitting stockings from Red Cross yarn. She was so small that she looked like an aged fairy. Unable to move from her chair, she knitted all day and all evening; sometimes Amelia heard her needles clicking

at night. All the little children in Coaltown had been sweatered and stockinged by Gran'ma. She looked anxiously at her daughter-in-law—Amelia had a hard time.

"I have a little peppermint candy put away," she said. "That will help."

From his high chair the year-old baby, still unnamed, lifted his voice. His howls said: "I'm hungry, that's what I am! I'm starving!"

Amelia threw her apron over her head and stepped out the door and along the side of the house. It was like walking in a tunnel, the piled snow was so deep. To her right towered the mammoth breaker and a veritable mountain of mined coal for which there was no market. Black against an orange sky, where hung the new moon like a golden thread, and Venus like a glittering gem, stood a row of fifty frame houses, all alike.

Moved by the impulse which had moved Amelia, four women appeared on doorsteps and at gates. Next door stood tall Grace Tanger, in dark blue Red Cross cotton cloth, which she had cut stylishly without a pattern. She was the only woman in Coaltown with a claim to beauty. She looked not at the breaker at which she appeared to look, but through it at the grim hill in whose depths her husband had met his death. When the mine opened, if it ever opened, other women would have men to work for them, but Grace would have no one: moreover, her home would be taken from her. Farther down the row stood Gwenny Thomas, a Welsh woman, wrapped in a red shawl, Irish Mrs. O'Hara in black, and

Mrs. Nuncio, part Mexican and part dear knows what, in dull orange.

"Where are the children?" asked Grace, in her clear, serious voice.

"The Lord knows," answered Mrs. O'Hara. "Not a sound do you hear."

"They're coastin'!" shouted O'Hara, from the end of the street. "Leave 'em play—what else can they do?"

Mothers' minds ran on the same track. "An' git appetites like houn' pups!" cried Mrs. O'Hara. "Go in, Grace Tanger, wid yer bare head!"

"Merry Chris'mass!" called a man's voice, and instantly Grace stood still and every other woman turned her head. In line with the row of dwellings and a little apart stood the Community House, a broad, squat building, some of its rooms on the street level, others running down the hill. Here under one roof were the store, the bunk rooms which accommodated forty men, the dining room where they ate, the lounging room where they played games and talked, the kitchen fitted with electric appliances run from the plant. The speaker was Michael Larson, a Swede, formerly a cook. He stood on the step, a giant with long, pendant yellowish mustaches. His English, learned from Italian laborers, was the queerest English ever heard.

He was now an important person; the departing superintendent had put him in charge not of the property alone but of the ten families who stayed because they had no place to go. "They

can at least keep warm. Let them have the coal they need. The Red Cross will give flour and the company will furnish a per capita allowance of food."

"If only the teacher could stay!" sighed Coaltown. But the teacher was invited to take a vacation without pay through December, January, February, and March. Hitherto a home missionary had preached in the schoolhouse on alternate Sundays; now even he failed to appear.

His greeting answered by silence, the Swede called "Merry Chris'mass," again, with exactly the same result. Then a shocking thing happened. This second blow Amelia gave to herself. Of all the dwellers in Coaltown, she was most careful of her speech, most ambitious for her children; she had even dreamed of sending them thirty miles to high school. In her desperation she became suddenly another person. "Oh, yeah?" she said loudly, sarcastically and savagely.

"'Chris'mass'!" mocked Mrs. O'Hara, quick to imitate. "What's that?"

"'Chris'mass'!" scoffed black-browed Gwenny Thomas. "That's done for!"

Imperturbable, unaffected by jeers, stood the Swede. "Four o'clock tomorrow da treat," he called. "Eferybody promp'."

"'Treat'!" mocked Gwenny. "A dry orange and a stick of stale candy!"

Horrified at herself, Amelia went into the house. "I'm ashamed," she thought. "The Evil One tempts me."

The six children came with a roar—Mary and Harry, Doris and Belle, Raymond and Melvin. Amelia gave them bread, spread thinly with apple butter, and large portions of mush spread with nothing, and Gran'ma gave each a peppermint drop. Gran'ma sat knitting and knitting; her clever hands seemed to fly. Amelia determined that she would keep all the children at home. They ought not to coast any more, nor ought they torture other mothers as frantic as she was. Sometimes they visited the Community House, but lately the Swede locked the doors and apparently went to bed early. "I could read them the Christmas story," she thought "And Gran'ma could tell about Christmas back in Ohio."

As she ate supper, she changed her mind. "I can't stand the noise," she thought. Never had the children been so difficult to manage. "Where are you going?" she asked when the oldest four put on their sweaters. "Coasting," they said, and were gone.

Bill went to play checkers in the engine house; she put Melvin and Raymond and the baby and Gran'ma to bed; then she lay down. "I go to no treat," she thought. "They don't dare for shame's sake let us die; that's all the responsibility they feel. Treat! They'll take whatever they give off the dole." When she heard the children laughing she meant to look at the clock, but she was too tired. "Idle," she thought. "No schooling, no trades."

Deep down in her heart she was not so despairing as she was on the surface. "Gran'ma'll have presents. She'll have little things put away, she'll have made something for each one."

She woke early, dressed quietly, and went down to the kitchen.

The cold was bitter; the fires, two or three in each house, did not last through the long night. It used to be that the mine whistle wakened everyone; now there was no whistle. Let Bill sleep and forget. She avoided looking at the kitchen mantel—that was where Gran'ma, aided by Bill, placed her gifts. She laid kindling in the stove, lighted it, and tipped up the coal scuttle.

It was not until she turned the dough out on the baking board that she lifted her eyes. For the third time, her heart stopped. There was nothing on the mantel but the clock! She drew in her breath. "She has nothing. Everything's gone. Gwenny's right—Christmas is done for. I'm glad I answered the Swede as I did. Not a step will I go to the treat. Treat!"

She served her family a late breakfast of boiled hominy. "Dinner at four," she announced grimly. "Two meals on Christmas."

With one voice Mary and Harry, Doris and Belle, Melvin and Raymond protested. "That's the time for the treat!" The baby added howl.

"Well, you pack yourselves right back here after your treat."

"Ain't you goin', Mom?"

"No, I'm not."

Her fourth shock was that of awful fright. The day was clear as a bell, the bright cold still held, the hills were like glass. At half-past three she groaned, "What'll I feed 'em, Mother?"

Gran'ma's answer seemed almost insulting to a person of intelligence. "The Lord will provide."

"Oh, yeah?" Amelia lifted her shawl from the nail behind the

door. "I'm going to walk out. The baby'll sleep till I get back."

Gran'ma said nothing; she always knew when to say nothing.

Amelia walked to the end of the street. "The Lord will provide—oh, yeah?" said she.

Presently the road turned away from the hill, and instantly she was in a drift to her knees. "No doubt he's awake and yelling," she thought without tenderness, and turned back. The snow was no longer a dead white; near buildings there were lavender and purple shadows, and in the open there were orange and yellow reflections. Soon the moon would hang like a golden thread and Venus would glitter like a gem. She saw men, women, and children hurrying toward the Community House. "Not me!" she thought. "The poor idiots!"

Opening her door, she stood terrified. For five years Gran'ma had not taken a step; she was tied to her chair as if by chains. On summer evenings Bill and Harry lifted her, chair and all, to the porch. Now, with the weather at zero, Gran'ma was gone. Moreover, the baby, able only to totter, was gone too. Amelia sank down in a chair.

Before she caught her breath, fright gave place to anger. "They're at the treat!" Bill, no doubt, got help and took them; he was soft-hearted; he could never stand up for his rights. Of course the children would go, and of course everyone else in Coaltown would go. But not Gran'ma, risking her life! Or the baby! "I'll get *him* back in a jiffy!"

Excited as she was, she did not forget to put coal on the fire.

She ran out the door and up the street. The shades at the Community House were raised and there were wreaths in the windows. She stepped into the lounging room and stood gasping.

First of all, she saw eyes—Gran'ma and Bill and Mary and Harry and Doris and Belle and Melvin and Raymond turned necks already stiff with turning. "There she is!" cried three or four of her children. The baby uttered a shriek. The lounging room was decked with boughs of blue spruce from the canyon five miles away, and packed with human beings. "She's here!" yelled a dozen voices. Gwenny Thomas' oldest boy leaped to the folding doors which shut off the dining room and pounded upon them. "She's here!" The big Swede opened the doors. "Merry Chris'mass!" he said. "Now slow! Gran'ma first, den laties an' babies."

"Ain't Gran'ma a lady?" demanded Mrs. O'Hara hysterically.

The Swede ignored this witticism. "Who pushes, gets gizzards."

"Gizzards!" mocked Coaltown.

"Gizzards," said the Swede, his mustaches quivering.

In the dining room was Grace Tanger, her fine body erect, her eyes smiling, and little dark Gwenny Thomas, who had declared that Christmas was done for. The turkeys were carved, the mashed potatoes and the corn and the stuffing and the onions were served. Adult hearts actually stopped beating; young hearts throbbed all the faster. "Wow!" shrieked some. "Lookit!" screamed others. "I've got a drumstick!"—"Get on to the white meat!"

"You pray, Gran'ma," ordered the Swede.

Gran'ma prayed earnestly and with appropriate brevity.

"Go slow," ordered the Swede. "Leetle bit bites. Chew mooch."

The Swede was now here, now there. Once he was out of the room a long time, but when the children called for him he was standing by the pantry door. He had made not only mince pie; he had made ice cream with condensed milk, the best Coaltown ever tasted. He directed everyone to stay in place until the tables were cleared; then he pushed the tables back against the wall and faced the chairs toward the lounging room. Standing on each side of the broad doors, Harry Brodhead and Millie Tanger rolled them back.

"Oh!" cried Amelia. Oh's, ah's, laughter—the confusion was greater than any which ever tortured Amelia's ears in her own house. There stood a blue spruce, pushed in on a low-wheeled platform. "We helped trim it! We helped get it!" shrieked forty adolescent voices. "I have a speech!" screamed a young Thomas. "I can sing a song!" yelled an O'Hara.

Under the tree lay at least forty pairs of stockings—Gran'ma knew whose feet were most nearly bare. The teacher, who was to have three months' vacation without pay and who had little enough at the best, sent a thick storybook, and her hand was to be discerned in much of the program.

When the children's speechmaking and the singing were over, the Swede stood up. The children had spoken of stockings, hang-

ing in a row, of gifts, of sleigh rides, of Santa Claus; he spoke of the Christ child. "I vill sing a Chris'mass song. In Swedish." The song had only two stanzas, but he could scarcely reach the end.

"I know that in English!" said Gran'ma. "'Away in a manger, no crib for His bed.'" "An' I! An' I," cried most of the men and women. The Swede swallowed a few times.

"I gotta make a speech for da Companee. Da Companee say, 'Michael, make a Chris'mass.' So I make a Chris'mass. Now Chris'mass bring da idee. I gotta lotta idee. No school for two mont'. I have school. I teacha young laties to cook. All here on my stove. No home folk need eat cooking." No comedian had ever a more instantaneous or hysterical response. "I gotta 'nother idee. Gran'ma teacha young laties to knit. Young laties knitta da sweater for beau."

"Ha, ha!" shrieked Coaltown. The women covered their mouths with their hands, men slapped each other on the back.

"I gotta idee. Mis' Tanger, she teacha young laties to sew. I gotta 'nother idee. Mis' Nuncio she teacha da laties da fancywork. She cut out da hole and sew in da spider and da crab." Again Coaltown shouted. "I gotta idee. Thomas, he teacha da boys to hammer an' saw. How about?"

"Fine," shouted Bill Brodhead, breaking his silence. His voice had an odd sound, as though he strove for but did not quite achieve cheerfulness. What of the men? he seemed to say.

The Swede took a folded paper from his pocket, handling it as

though it were spun glass. "I gotta letter," he said. "'Dear Larson,' it say. 'On January 1, we begin ship little coal. Approx' tree day a week work for each man in January. Estimate necessary repairs.'"

"Repairs on what?" asked Bill Brodhead quickly.

The Swede opened his arms in a wide gesture. "Breaker, engine house, everyt'ing. It say too, "Merry Chris'mass!'"

Brodhead drew his sleeve across his eyes. "Ah!" sighed mothers and fathers.

Gran'ma traveled home as she had come—in the Swede's arms; rolled in three quilts, she made a great bundle. Bill carried the baby, and Melvin and Raymond trotted sleepily in the rear. Venus had vanished and the moon hung just above the horizon. Amelia stayed with Grace Tanger and Gwenny Thomas and the Mexican woman to do the dishes.

"You dirtied 'em, Swede," said Gwenny gaily. "We'll wash 'em." Again and again the dumb waiter creaked to the kitchen. Down the shaft with it came shouts, the patting of feet, and loud victrola music.

The shouts increased in intensity. "He's back—you can tell that," said Amelia indulgently. The Swede came down the steps; suddenly she faced him and the women. "What is there about Christmas?" she asked, the tears running down her cheeks.

The Swede looked smilingly round the little room. "My, I lika see da work gittin' done! I gotta idee about Chris'mass. At Chris'mass everyt'ing start fresh. Leetle baby come, heart swells up, gets soft. Everyt'ing new, fresh. New heart, new hope. God say, 'Now try again!' Dat my idee."

"He says, 'Now try again, you poor boobs,'" said Gwenny, weeping.

The Swede shook his head. "He not dat rough. He say, "Poor leetle babies!"

The Swede walked home with his assistants. It was nine o'clock, the moon was gone, the star-filled sky had a greater glory. He dropped Gwenny at her door, Mrs. Nuncio at hers, Grace Tanger at hers, then he crossed the street with Amelia Brodhead.

"Bill would be glad to see you," said Amelia. "Come in."

The Swede ignored her invitation. "You smart woman," he said. "House clean, children clean, Gran'ma happy. Soon you get pretty again."

Amelia laughed. "Not very smart and often very cross and never pretty."

"I gotta 'nother idee," said the Swede. "Mis' Tanger all alone. Lotta children. Nice children. Eferybody but she got man to earn wages. I shy. You t'ink she take me?"

Amelia's brain seemed to spin like a wheel; now one recollection was uppermost, now another. She saw Grace's fine figure, her deep bright eyes. Her face had been flushed, she seemed a little excited. The Swede was handsome, he was kind, he was steady as could be. "I gotta idea she might," she gasped.

"Now da time?" asked the Swede. "New business for me."

"Now!" urged Amelia. "This very minute!"

"Goodbye!" said the Swede, already halfway across the street. "Merry Chris'mass."

"Merry Christmas!" called Amelia, with all her heart.

Which of the Nine?

Maurus Jókai

translated by Monique Jean

Many waters cannot quench love;
Rivers cannot wash it away.
If one were to give all the
wealth of his house for love,
it would be utterly scorned.

SONG OF SONGS 8:7, NIV

In the city of Budapest there lived a poor shoemaker who simply couldn't make ends meet. Not because people had suddenly decided to give up wearing boots, nor because the city council had passed an ordinance directing that shoes be sold at half price, nor even because his work was not satisfactory. Indeed, the good man did such excellent work that his customers actually complained that they couldn't wear out anything he had once sewed together. He had plenty of customers who paid him promptly and well enough; not one of them had run away without settling his bill. And yet Cobbler John couldn't make both ends meet.

The reason was that the good Lord had blessed him all too plentifully with nine children, all of them as healthy as acorns.

Then, one day, as if Cobbler John hadn't already had trouble enough, his wife died. Cobbler John was left alone in this world with nine children. Two or three of them were going to school; one or two were being tutored; one had to be carried around; gruel had to be cooked for the next; another had to be fed, the next one dressed, yet another washed. And on top of all this he

had to earn a living for all of them. Verily, brethren, this was a big job—just try it in case you doubt it!

When shoes were made for them, nine had to be made all at once; when bread was sliced, nine slices had to be cut all at one time. When beds were made ready, the entire room between window and door became one single bed, full of little and big blond and brunette heads.

"Oh my dear Lord God, how Thou hast blessed me," the good artisan often sighed while even after midnight he still worked and hammered away at his lasts in order to feed the bodies of so many souls, stopping occasionally to chide now one, now another tossing restlessly in a dream. Nine they were—a round number nine. But thanks be to the Lord, there was still no cause for complaint, because all nine were healthy, obedient, beautiful, and well-behaved, blessed with sound bodies and stomachs. And rather should there be nine pieces of bread than one bottle of medicine; rather nine side by side than coffins between them. But none of Cobbler John's children had the slightest intention of dying. It was already fated that all nine of them should fight their way through life and not yield their places to anybody. Neither rain nor snow nor dry bread would ever hurt them.

On Christmas Eve, Cobbler John returned late from his many errands. He had delivered all sorts of finished work and had collected a little money which he had to use to buy supplies and to pay for their daily needs. Hurrying homeward, he saw stands on

every street corner, loaded with golden and silver lambs and candy dolls which pushcart women were selling as gifts for well-behaved children. Cobbler John stopped before one or two of the carts.... Maybe he ought to buy something.... What? For all nine? That would cost too much. Then for just one? And make the others envious? No, he'd give them another kind of Christmas present: a beautiful and good one, one that would neither break nor wear out, and which all could enjoy together and not take away from each other.

"Well, children! One, two, three, four... are you all here?" he said when he arrived home within the circle of his family of nine. "Do you know that this is Christmas Eve? A holiday, a very gay holiday. Tonight we do not work, we just rejoice!"

The children were so happy to hear that they were supposed to rejoice that they almost tore down the house.

"Wait now! Let's see if I can't teach you that beautiful song I know. It's a very beautiful song. I have saved it to give it to you all as a Christmas present."

The little ones crawled noisily into their father's lap and up on his shoulders, and waited eagerly to hear the lovely song.

"Now what did I tell you? If you are good children... just stand nicely in line!... there... the bigger ones over here and the smaller ones next to them." He stood them in a row like organ pipes, letting the two smallest ones stay on his lap.

"And now—silence! First I'll sing it through, then you join

in." Taking off his green cap and assuming a serious, pious expression, Cobbler John began to sing the beautiful melody: "On the blessed birth of Our Lord Jesus Christ...."

The bigger boys and girls learned it after one rendition, though the smaller ones found it a bit more difficult. They were always off key and out of rhythm. But after a while they all knew it. And there could be no more joyous sound than when all the nine thin little voices sang together that glorious song of the angels on that memorable night. Perhaps the angels were still singing it when the melodious voices of nine innocent souls prayed for an echo from above. For surely there is gladness in heaven over the song of children.

But there was less gladness immediately above them.

There, a bachelor was living all by himself in nine rooms. In one he sat, in the other one he slept, in the third one he smoked his pipe, in the fourth he dined, and who knows what he did in all the others? This man had neither wife nor children but more money than he could count. Sitting in room number eight that night, this rich man was wondering why life had lost its taste. Why did his soft spring bed give him no peaceful dreams? Then, from Cobbler John's room below, at first faintly but with ever-increasing strength, came the strains of a certain joy-inspiring song. At first he tried not to listen, thinking they would soon stop. But when they started all over for the tenth time, he could stand it no longer. Crushing out his expensive cigar, he went down in his dressing gown to the shoemaker's flat.

They had just come to the end of the verse when he walked in. Cobbler John respectfully got up from his three-legged stool and greeted the great gentleman.

"You are John, the cobbler, aren't you?" the rich man asked.

"That I am, and at your service, your Excellency. Do you wish to order a pair of patent leather boots?"

"That isn't why I came. How very many children you have!"

"Indeed, I have, Your Excellency—little ones and big ones. Quite a few mouths to feed!"

"And many more mouths when they sing! Look here, Master John—I'd like to do you a favor. Give me one of your children. I'll adopt him, educate him as my own son, take him traveling abroad with me, and make him into a gentleman. One day he'll be able to help the rest of you."

Cobbler John stared wide-eyed when he heard this. These were big words—to have one of his children made into a gentleman! Who wouldn't be taken by such an idea? Why, of course, he'd let him have one! What great good fortune! How could he refuse?

"Well, then, pick out one of them quickly, and let's get it over with," said the gentleman. Cobbler John started to choose.

"This one here is Alex. No, him I couldn't let go. He is a good student and I want him to become a priest. The next one? That's a girl, and of course Your Excellency doesn't want a girl. Little Ferenc? He already helps me with my work. I couldn't do without him. Johnny? There, there—he is named after me. I couldn't

very well give him away! Joseph? He is the image of his mother—it's as if I see her every time I look at him. This place wouldn't be the same without him. And the next is another girl—she wouldn't do. Then comes little Paul: he was his mother's favorite. Oh, my poor darling would turn in her grave if I gave him away. And the last two are too small—they'd be too much trouble for Your Excellency...."

He had reached the end of the line without being able to choose. Now he started all over; this time beginning with the youngest and ending with the oldest. But the result was still the same: he couldn't decide which one to give away because one was a dear to him as the other and he would miss them all.

"Come, my little ones—you do the choosing," he finally said. "Which one of you wants to go away to become a gentleman and travel in style? Come now, speak up! Who wants to go?"

The poor shoemaker was on the verge of tears as he asked them. But while he was encouraging them, the children slowly slipped behind their father's back, each taking hold of him, his hand, his leg, his coat, his leather apron, all hanging on to him, and hiding from the great gentleman. Finally Cobbler John couldn't control himself any longer. He knelt down, gathered them all into his arms and let his tears fall on their heads as they cried with him.

"It can't be done, Your Excellency! It can't be done. Ask of me anything in the world, but I can't give you a single one of my

children so long as the Lord God has given them to me."

The rich gentleman said that he understood, but that the shoemaker should do at least one thing for him: would he and his children please not sing anymore? And for this sacrifice he asked Cobbler John to accept one thousand florins.

Master John had never even heard the words, "One thousand florins," spoken, never in all his life. Now he felt the money being pressed into his hand.

His Excellency went back to his room and his boredom. And Cobbler John stood staring incredulously at the oddly shaped banknote. Then he fearfully locked it away in the wooden chest, put the key into his pocket and was silent. The little ones were silent, too. Singing was forbidden. The older children slumped moodily in their chairs, quieting the smaller ones by telling them they weren't allowed to sing anymore because it disturbed the fine gentleman upstairs. Cobbler John himself was silently walking up and down. Impatiently he pushed aside little Paul, the one who had been his wife's favorite, when the boy asked that he be taught again that beautiful song because he had already forgotten how it went.

"We aren't allowed to sing anymore!"

Then he sat down angrily at his bench and bent intently over his work. He cut and hammered and sewed until suddenly he caught himself humming: "On the blessed birth of Our Lord Jesus Christ...." He clapped his hand over his mouth. But then

all at once he was very angry. He banged the hammer down on the workbench, kicked his stool from under him, opened the chest, took out the thousand florin bill and ran up the stairs to His Excellency's apartment.

"Good, kind Excellency, I am your most humble servant. Please take back your money! Let it not be mine, but let us sing whenever we please, because to me and my children that is worth much more than a thousand florins."

With that he put the bill down on the table and rushed breathlessly back to his waiting family. He kissed them one after the other; and lining them up in a row just like organ pipes, he sat himself down on his low stool, and together they began to sing again with heart and soul: "On the blessed birth of Our Lord Jesus Christ...." They couldn't have been happier if they had owned the whole of the great big house.

But the one who owned the house was pacing through his nine rooms, asking himself how it was that those people down below could be so happy and full of joy in such a tiresome, boring world as this.

Christmas in the Cathedral

Elizabeth Goudge

And how blessed all those in whom you
live, whose lives become roads you travel;
They wind through lonesome valleys,
come upon brooks, discover cool springs
and pools brimming with rain!
God-traveled, these roads curve up the
mountain, and at the last turn—Zion!
God in full view!

PSALMS 84:5-7, *THE MESSAGE*

Every year, at half past five on Christmas Eve, the tower bell "Michael" lifted his great fist and struck the double quarter, and the Cathedral bells rang out. They pealed for half an hour all over the city, and in all the villages to which the wind carried the sound of the bells, they knew that Christmas had begun. People in the fen wrapped cloaks about them and went out of doors and stood looking towards the city. This year it was bitterly cold but the wind had swept the clouds away and the Cathedral on its hill towered up among the stars, light shining from its windows. Below it the twinkling city lights were like clustering fireflies about its feet. The tremendous bell music that was rocking the tower and pealing through the city was out here as lovely and far away as though it rang out from the stars themselves, and it caught at men's hearts. "Now 'tis Christmas," they said to each other, as their forebears had said for centuries past, looking towards the city on the hill and the great fane that was as much a part of their blood and bones as the fen itself. "'Tis Christmas," they said, and went back happy to their homes.

In the city, as soon as the bells started, everyone began to get ready. Then from nearly every house family parties came out and

made their way up the steep streets towards the Cathedral. Quite small children were allowed to stay up for the carol service, and they chattered like sparrows as they stumped along buttoned into their thick coats, the boys gaitered and mufflered, the girls with muffs and fur bonnets. It was the custom in the city to put lighted candles in the windows on Christmas Eve and their light, and the light of the street lamps, made of the street ladders of light leaning against the hill. The grownups found them to be Jacob's ladders tonight, easy to climb, for the bells and the children tugged them up.

Nearly everyone entered by the west door, for they loved the thrill of crossing the green under the moon and stars, and mounting the steps and gazing up at the west front, and then going in through the Porch of the Angels beneath Michael and the pealing bells. Some of them only came to the Cathedral on this one day in the year, but as they entered the nave they felt the impact of its beauty no less keenly than those who came often. It was always like a blow between the eyes, but especially at night, and especially on Christmas Eve when they were full of awe and expectation. There were lights in the nave but they could do no more than splash pools of gold here and there, they could not illumine the shadows above or the dim unlighted chantries and half-seen tombs. The great pillars soared into darkness and the aisles narrowed to twilight. Candles twinkled in the choir and the high altar with its flowers was ablaze with them, but all the myriad flames were no more than seed pearls embroidered on a dark

cloak. The great rood was veiled in shadow. All things alike went out into mystery. The crowd of tiny human creatures flowed up the nave and on to the benches. The sound of their feet, of their whispering voices and rustling garments, was lost in the vastness. The music of the organ flowed over them and they were still.

But a few came in through the south door and Tom Hochicorn gave them greeting as he stood bowing by his brazier. Albert Lee had worked quickly, had come by some charcoal and had it lighted and installed by the time the bells began to ring. He had sat on the bench chatting to old Tom for a while and then, as people began to arrive, he took fright and was all for escaping back to Swithins Lane, but old Tom grabbed him and held on with surprising strength. "Go inside, Bert," he commanded.

"What, me?" gasped Albert Lee. "In there? Not likely!"

"Why not, Bert?"

"Full of toffs," said Albert Lee. "'Ere, Tom, you leggo. I don't want to 'urt you."

"You won't see no toffs," said old Tom. "Not to notice. Just a lot of spotted ladybirds a-setting on the floor. That's all they look like in there. You go in, Bert. Not afraid, are you?"

"Afraid?" scoffed Albert Lee. "I ain't been afraid of nothink not since I was born."

"Go in, then," said Tom. He opened the door and motioned to Albert. "Look there. See that pillar? The one by the stove. There's a chair behind it. No one won't see you if you set behind

that pillar. If you look round it when you hear the Dean speaking you'll see him."

He had hold of Albert by his coat collar. Albert didn't want to make a scene or own himself afraid. He found himself inside with the door softly closed behind him. Sweating profusely he crept to the chair behind the pillar and sat down on its extreme edge. What a place! It was like old Tom had said. No one didn't notice you in here. You were too small. This was a terrible place! It was like night up there. But the door was near, and so was the homely-looking stove. For a while his eyes clung to the door, and then as the warmth of the stove flowed out to him his terror began to subside. It was nice and warm in his corner. No one couldn't see him. He'd sit for a while. The bells were pretty but he didn't like that great humming rumbling music that was sending tremors though his legs. Then it stopped, and the bells too, and there was silence, and then miles away he heard boys singing.

They came nearer and nearer, singing like the birds out in the fen in spring. One by one men's voices began to join in, and then the multitude of men and women whom he could scarcely see began to sing too. The sound grew, soaring up the the great darkness overhead. It pulled him to his feet. He didn't know the words and he didn't know the music but he had sung with the Romany people in his boyhood, sitting round the campfire in the drove, and he'd been quick to pick up a tune. He was now. He dared not use his coarsened voice but the music sang in his blood like sap rising in a tree. When the hymn ended there was a strange

rustling sound, like leaves stirring all over a vast forest. It startled him at first until he realized that it was all the toffs kneeling down. He knelt too, his tattered cap in his hands, and the slight stir of his movement was drawn into the music of all the other movements. For the forest rustling was also music and that too moved in his blood. There was silence again and far away he heard the Dean's voice raised in the bidding prayer. He could not distinguish a word but the familiar voice banished the last of his fear. When the prayer ended he said Amen as loudly as any and was no longer conscious of loneliness. From then until the end he was hardly conscious even of himself.

There were not many who were. It was that which made this particular Christmas Eve carol service memorable above all others in the city's memory. The form of it was the same as always. The familiar hymns and carols followed each other in the familiar order; the choir sang "Wonderful, Counsellor, the Mighty God, the everlasting Father, the Prince of Peace," as gloriously as ever but not more so, for they always put the last ounce into it; the difference was that instead of the congregation enjoying themselves enjoying the carol service they were enjoying the carol service. They were not tonight on the normal plane of human experience. When they had climbed the Jacob's ladders of the lighted streets from the city to the Cathedral they had climbed up just one rung higher than they usually did.

There was another difference. The form of this service was the same as always but the emphasis was different. Generally the peak

of it all was the anthem, but tonight it was the Christmas gospel, read as always by the Dean.

Adam Ayscough walked with a firm step to the lectern, put on his eyeglasses, and found the place. As he and Elaine had left the Deanery to go to the Cathedral he had been in great fear, for he had not known he would do it. "All shall be well and all manner of thing shall be well." He cleared his throat. "The first verse of the first chapter of the gospel according to St. John," he said. His sight, he found, was worse than usual and the page was misty. But it was no matter for he knew the chapter by heart. He raised his head and looked out over the congregation. "In the beginning was the Word, and the Word was with God."

His voice was like a raucous trumpet, it had such power behind it. The people listened without movement, but though they had all come filled with thankfulness because he would be here tonight they were not thinking of him as they had thought of him on other Christmas Eves, thinking how ugly he was, how awkward, but yet how in place there in the lectern, looming up above them in his strange rugged strength; they were thinking only of what he was saying. "The Word was made flesh and dwelt among us." Was it really true? Could it be true? If it was true, then the rood up there was the king-pin that kept all things in perpetual safety and they need never fear again. To many that night Adam Asycough's speaking of the Christmas gospel was a bridge between doubt and faith, perhaps because it came to them with such a splendid directness. He stood for a moment looking out

over the people, then left the lectern and went back to his stall. His sight had been too dim to see them when he looked at them and he had no knowledge that he had been of service to them.

Nor, when at the conclusion of the service the Bishop and clergy, the choir and the whole congregation, flocked down to the west end of the nave for the traditional singing of "Now thank we all our God," did he know that his presence with them all was one of the chief causes of their thanksgiving. But when the Bishop had blessed them, and the clergy and choir had turned to go to their vestries, he did what no Dean had ever done before—moving to the west door, he stood there to greet the people as they went out. To break with tradition in this manner was unlike him, for he revered tradition, yet he found himself moving to the west door.

He had no idea that quite so many people as this came to the Cathedral on Christmas Eve. Surely nearly the whole city was here. Most of them only dared to smile at him shyly as they passed by, but some bolder spirits spoke to him, saying they were glad he was better and returning his good wishes when he wished them a happy Christmas. To his astonished delight almost all those who in the last few months had become so especially dear to him, like his own small flock of sheep, were among those who gave him a special greeting.

Bella was there, in her cherry-red outfit, clasping her doll. "She would come," her grandmother whispered to him, "though it's long past her bedtime, and she would bring her doll. I knew it

was not right but I could not prevent it." Mrs. Havelock was looking extremely tired and the Dean took her hand to reassure her. Bella, who had been looking as smugly solid as a stationary robin, suddenly became airborne and darted off into the night. Mrs. Havelock, abruptly dropping the Dean's hand, fled in pursuit.

Mr. Penny was there, bowing very shyly as he passed, and Ruth with her wise calm smile and little Miss Throstle of the umbrella shop. Albert Lee was there, borne along by the crowd as an integral part of it and quite comfortable in his non-entity, and yet bold as well as comfortable for he was one of those who paused to wish the Dean a happy Christmas. Polly and Job were there, as he had known they would be, but they smiled at him as though from a vast distance, and he was glad of it. They were in their own world. Polly wore her bonnet with the cherry-coloured ribbons and her left hand lay on Job's right arm in the traditional manner of those who are walking out. She had left her glove off on purpose that the world might see her ring.

With them was Miss Peabody, looking not so much ill as convalescent. She was one of those for whom despair, to which she had lived so near for so long, had receded during the reading of the Christmas gospel. Yet she would have slipped past the Dean unnoticed had he not stopped her and taken her hand. "A happy Christmas, Miss Peabody," he said cheerfully, as though there had been no clock. "I am obliged to you for coming tonight. Much obliged. God bless you."

Back in the Deanery again there were many matters to attend

to and it was not until late in the evening that he went to his study to finish writing his Christmas sermon. He turned back to the beginning of it, to refresh his mind as to what he had already written, and as he read he was in despair. It was a terrible sermon for its Christmas purpose of joy and love. It was academic, abstruse, verbose. Why was it that he could write a book but could not write a sermon? He told himself that a sermon was a thing of personal contact, and in personal contacts he had always failed most miserably. Already, as he turned the pages of this most wretched sermon, he could feel the wave of boredom and dislike that always seemed to beat up in his face when he tried to preach, and he shrank miserably within himself. Nevertheless the sermon had to be written and it had to be preached and he picked up his pen, dipped it in the ink, and began to write.

But presently he found to his dismay that he could not see what he wrote. He turned back to the earlier pages and found they were as blurred as the page of the gospels had been when he stood in the lectern. He realized that he was too tired to prepare this sermon, too tired to sit here any longer at his desk. Fear took hold of him. This dimming of his sight had not mattered this evening, for he had known what he had to say, but in the pulpit it would be fatal, for he had never been able to preach in any other way than by reading aloud from the written page. The gospel he had known by heart. "By heart." It seemed to his bewilderment and fatigue as though a voice had spoken. A great simplicity had come into his life these last months, a grace that had been given

to him with the friendship of humble people. Could he tomorrow preach from his heart and not his intellect? Could he look upon his heart with his inward eyes and speak what he found written upon it? A man's heart was the tablet of God, who wrote upon it what he willed. He took up the manuscript of his sermon and tore it across, flinging the fragments into the wastepaper basket.

Then he lit the candle that stood upon a side table, put out the lamp and went out into the darkened hall. When there was much work to be done he often went to bed very late and by his command no servant waited up for him. He climbed the stairs slowly with his candle, and as he climbed the clamour of the bells broke out once more. It was midnight, the hour of Christ's birth. At the top of the stairs there was a window. He put his candle down on the sill and stood for a moment in prayer. They he opened the old casement a few inches and the sound of the bells swept in to him on a breath of cold air. He closed the window again and saw that a snowflake lay on his hand.

The congregation in the Cathedral on Christmas morning at matins was not the large one of Christmas Eve, when the carol service was the only one in the city. It was the usual Sunday congregation, but larger than was customary because it was Christmas Day. It was a distinguished congregation, containing all the élite of the city. As the Dean walked in procession to his

stall past the long rows of well-dressed, well-fed people, his nose was assailed by delicate perfumes, the scent of rich furs and shoe polish, and in spite of his happiness panic rose in him again, and this time he could not subdue it. How could he have imagined that he could preach a simple extempore sermon to people such as these? They would be outraged. He would bring shame upon the Bishop and his learned brethren of the chapter, upon the Cathedral and upon Elaine. He did not know how to preach extempore. Nervous and anxious as he always was when he had to speak in public he had never attempted such a thing. He was so dismayed that by the time he reached the choir his hands were clammy and trembling. Then, as he settled into the Dean's stall like a statue into its niche, reassurance came to him from the great joyous Cathedral. He was as much a humble part of it as the shepherd under the miserere seat, as the knights on their tombs and the saints and angels in the windows, as the very stones and beams of its structure. They all had their function to perform in its Christmas adoration and not the humblest or the least would be allowed to fall.

As the Te Deum soared to the roof, to the sky, and took wings to the four corners of the earth, he felt himself built into the fabric of the singing stones and the shouting exulting figures all about him. The stamping of the unicorns, the roaring of the lions, and the noise the angels made with their trumpets and cymbals almost drowned the thunder of the organ. The knights sang on their tombs and the saints in their windows, and the

homely men and boys and birds were singing under the miserere seats. Adam Ayscough was not surprised. He had had a similar experience long ago as a child, although until this moment he had forgotten it. The human brain was an organ of limitation. It restricted a grown man's consciousness of the exterior world to what was practically useful to him. It was like prison walls. Without them possibly he could not have concentrated sufficiently upon the task he had to do. But in childhood and old age the prison walls were of cloudy stuff and there were occasional rents in them.

The tremendous music sang on in him after the Te Deum had ended but it did not prevent him from doing efficiently all that he had to do. He made the right responses, he walked to the lectern to read the second lesson and returned to his stall again, and during the hymn before the sermon he knelt in his stall to pray as he always did. But today he did not pray for strength to mount the huge pulpit under the sounding board, for he hardly remembered it. He prayed for the city.

Yet when he was in the pulpit he instinctively steeled himself against that wave of boredom and resignation that always rose and broke over him when he stood above the distant congregation like Punch on his stage. It did not come. There was no distance. They were all as close to him as his own body. His sight was better today and he looked down at them for a moment; at Elaine in her pew, her head bent and her hands in her muff, at Mary Montague, at Mr. Penny over to his right, quite close to him.... The Dean forgot all about the well-dressed critical men

and women who had so alarmed him while he walked past them.

He took his text from Dean Rollard's psalm, the sixty-eighth, "God is the Lord by whom we escape death." He spoke of love, and a child could have understood him. He said that only in the manger and upon the cross is love seen in its maturity, for upon earth the mighty strength of love has been unveiled once only. On earth, among men, it is seldom more than a seed in the hearts of those who choose it. If it grows at all it is no more than a stunted and sometimes harmful thing, for its true growth and purging are beyond death. There it learns to pour itself out until it has no self left to pour. Then, in the hollow of God's hand into which it has emptied itself, it is his own to all eternity. If there were no life beyond death, argued the Dean, there could be no perfecting of love, and no God, since he is himself that life and love. It is by love alone that we escape death, and love alone is our surety for eternal life. If there were no springtime there would be no seeds. The small brown shell, the seed of an apple tree in bloom, is evidence for the sunshine and the singing of the birds.

He came down from the pulpit and walked back to his stall and fitted comfortably into his niche in the fabric. Presently, when the last hymn had been sung, he went up to the altar and blessed the people.

All over the city men and women and children poured out of the chapels and churches exclaiming at the beauty of the day. It

all looked as pretty as a picture, they said. The frost kept the sparkling snow from slipping away from roofs and chimney pots, but it was not too cold to spoil the sunshine. There was no wind. On their way home, whenever a distant view opened out, they could pause and enjoy it without having to shiver. The stretch of the snow-covered fen almost took their breath away, it was so beautiful under the blue arc of the sky. It was like the sea when it turns to silver under the dazzle of the sun. When they turned and looked up at the Cathedral its snow-covered towers seemed to rise to an immeasurable height. Then a wonderful fragrance assailed their nostrils. In steam-filled kitchens the windows had been opened now that the day was warming up. The turkeys and baked potatoes and plum puddings were also warming up and in another forty minutes would have reached the peak of their perfection. Abruptly Christmas Day swung over like a tossed coin. The silver and blue of bells and hymns and angels went down with a bang and was replaced by the red and gold of flaming plum puddings and candled trees. Everyone huried home as quickly as they could.

Christmas Day at the Deanery was one of the busiest of the year. When the morning services were over there was the ritual of the Christmas dinner, to which the Dean insisted that Elaine invite all the lonely people connected with the Close, such as bachelor minor canons and widows of defunct Cathedral dignitaries. This was usually something of an ordeal for all concerned but today not even the sight of the vast dead turkey could depress

the Dean, and old Mrs. Ramsey, whose terrifying privilege it was to sit upon his right, found him almost a genial host. When the guests had gone Elaine dissolved upon the sofa, but the Dean went out to visit the old men at the almshouses until it was time for evensong. Then there was a late tea, followed by the ceremony of the servants' Christmas tree. The difficult occasion had never seemed so happy. The servants almost forgot their shyness in their pleasure at seeing the Dean looking so much better. Elaine had never been so successful in disguising her boredom or the Dean in overcoming his trepidation. Afterwards, against better judgment, the Dean went round to the choir school Christmas tree as was his custom on Christmas Day; boys were his delight. The servants considered that Cook was in the right of it when she remarked that the boys should have made do with the Archdeacon this year. They'd scarcely have noticed the difference, not with their stomachs full.

Elaine went to bed dirctly after supper, her husband carrying her candle for her to her room.

"Are you very tired, my dear?" he asked her. "It has been a long day for you."

"Not so tired as usual," she said, pulling off her rings and dropping them on her dressing-table, and she added softly, looking away from him, "It has been a happy Christmas Day. I liked your sermon, Adam."

She had never said that before and his heart seemed to make a physical movement of joy. "It is true, Elaine," he said. "All I said

so haltingly is true. I'm glad you liked it. Good night, my dear. Sleep well."

She lifted her face and as he kissed her smooth cool cheek he felt suddenly that he could not leave her. He wanted to ask if he might sit in her armchair for a little while, in her warm scented room, and watch her brush her hair. It was years since he had seen her glorious hair down on her shoulders. But her eyes were drowning in sleep and he feared to weary her. He tiptoed from her room and closed the door softly behind him.

He went into his study, where the lamp had been lighted for him. He was deeply grateful that the labour of the last two days was now accomplished, and most thankful to find himself so well. He was abysmally tired, but he did not feel ill. He would work for a little longer before he went to bed.

He opened a deep drawer in his table and took out two piles of papers. One was the manuscript of his book and the other the architectural plans. The unfinished book cried out to him in its plight but he put it to one side. It was himself and so must be denied. For the hundredth time he unfolded all the plans and opened them before him. They were dog-eared now, and stained in several places, for they had been through so many hands and had been argued over so hotly for so long. And now it was all to do again. Tomorrow he would start the fight once more. He thought of it with dread, but that cancer could not be left in the body of the city. He remembered Dean Rollard singing the sixty-eighth psalm. "This is God's hill, in which it pleaseth him to

dwell." With what grief must God look upon the North Gate slums, and the rotting human bodies there. The Dean pulled a piece of paper towards him and wrote out the words in his fine handwriting, laying it upon the plan of the city. Then upon another piece of paper he began to calculate the cost of demolition and rebuilding all over again. If he could only get expenditure down a little he might meet less opposition. But he feared he had many enemies. In past years, stung nearly to madness by the sufferings of the poor, he had forced through reforms with too much anger and too much contempt for the oppressors. He was a gentler man now, but it was too late. Yet for an hour he went on working until the figures blurred and his gold pencil slipped from his hand.

"I must go to bed," he thought, and tried to get up from his chair. Then it came again, the rising panic in his blood, the constriction of his throat, as though a rope were being drawn tighter and tighter about it, a roaring in the ears and the agonizing struggle for breath. He did not feel the joy this time, for it was too bad, but a great voice cried out in the crashing blackness of his mind, "Blessed be God."

THE INNKEEPER

Douglas Livingstone

About that time Caesar Augustus ordered a census to be taken throughout the Empire. This was the first census when Quirinius was governor of Syria. Everyone had to travel to his own ancestral hometown to be accounted for. So Joseph went from the Galilean town of Nazareth up to Bethlehem in Judah, David's town, for the census. As a descendant of David, he had to go there. He went with Mary, his fiancée, who was pregnant.

While they were there, the time came for her to give birth. She gave birth to a son, her firstborn. She wrapped him in a blanket and laid him in a manger, because there was no room in the hostel.

LUKE 2:1-7, *THE MESSAGE*

Gaius sighed wearily. Outside the air was fresher. In the room he had just left the voices were loud. The night air muted the sound. Lights flickered in the windows of rooms opening onto the court. But the clear stars were not dimmed. He thought of the mountains where the air would be fresher still, cooler, sharper. Sitting in the quiet of the hills with the warmth of the dying fire would make a man content. He sighed again. Perhaps someday he could afford a manager, and, then, time with the pastured flocks and nights under the stars.

A pounding on the heavy door brought him back to his present responsibilities. As the pounding continued he called out, "Yes, I'm coming." But he did not hurry. The place was full anyway. This census business was beginning to tire him. A full house had its financial advantages, but demands of it week after week seemed more than it was worth. The help grumbled with overwork. He had not had a single afternoon in over a month to get away from the city and into the hills. A man had to have time alone, to relax, to renew himself with the energy of the earth through his feet. No, the Roman census with the increased business it brought was no blessing to him. He opened the small window in the door. There were six men on horseback. Immediately a voice commanded, "You. Be quick. Open the door."

"I'm sorry, sir," Gaius answered, ignoring the order. "We don't have a single room. Even the chair by our fire has been claimed."

"Let us in. There must be room somewhere. We can't stay in the streets."

Gaius should have left the door firmly shut. He knew that. But it wouldn't be safe for anyone to wander the streets this late. He hesitated, and was lost, though he began, "Have you tried…"

"We've tried everywhere," cut in the impatient speaker. "Let us into your courtyard, if nowhere else."

Gaius unbarred the door, but he stood in the doorway regarding the group. Three of the men looked as though they might be of some importance. The other three he took for slaves. The speaker dismounted and made to enter around Gaius. The innkeeper still hesitated and then turned to lead the men into the court. How could he leave them to the streets all night? he argued with himself.

Indicating a corner of the yard where they could sleep, he led the slaves and their horses to the stables. The smell of the warm beasts and the heavy scent of fresh hay greeted him. Contentment seeped into him as he helped the slaves settle the horses in. Animals seldom had trouble making room for more, he mused.

He lingered in the stable. Here was a society he loved. The years as an innkeeper slipped away. He was a boy—tagging along with his uncle to the pastures, unaware as yet of the complexities of the world of adult responsibility. All there was for him was the hills; the hills where he came to know the stupidity of sheep and the danger from a hungry predator; the hills of fierce storms and whims of wind that shoved clouds about the burning sky. Sitting beside a pool pulling brambles from a sheep's coat, or gazing at the sun sinking below the horizon—there he had known satisfaction. That was his real life; hours of solitude, days of reflection. Sheep were only animals, but they were capable of showing affection. Their nuzzles of appreciation were better payment than the silver paid for a night's lodging. The greedy hunger of a new lamb at its mother's tits had made him happy as he watched. He could still feel the pressure of the orphan lamb he had spoiled and petted, insistent against his leg for attention. And he had never forgotten the shock and sickness he felt when he came across a half-eaten carcass the first time. The blood had been so red against the white wool. Such was the violence of the hills, but it was part of the whole scheme of being—of living and dying. He had felt at home in the mountains and the cycles of their years.

What strange things chart a man's destiny. Marrying Suzanne, confident he could forget his Roman patrimony and the problems that caused with his Jewish grandparents, forget the harsh sound of soldiers' feet on the cobbled streets, forget the tiring

rush of the city. A shepherd forever, until the sudden death of Suzanne's father, and in a single night his life was redrawn. He and Suzanne had moved into the life of her father, and his father had followed. Only occasionally was he bitter, less so as the years passed; but the longing for the life of the hills never left him.

He heard a commotion in the courtyard. Sighing again, he turned from his reverie and became innkeeper again. The voices were muffled, but he could hear a tentative knocking over the growls of the men in the yard. Gaius hated turning people away more than the fatigue of serving their needs. People weren't able to take care of themselves in the streets in these times. The luxuries of civilization exacted their price. When the three men saw him, they eased their grumbles and turned to the wall. The knocking, to his aggravation, continued.

Gaius crossed the court and opened the window. Peering out he saw two figures, a taller one supporting someone bent over. Cautiously he unbarred the door. If this were a ruse there were enough strong arms at hand to stop any robbers.

"How can I help you? I haven't a room left in the place. There are people sleeping here in the yard." They he added apologetically, "The census, you know."

"Yes, the census." The voice hinted of great weariness, but it was controlled. "If you could let us even stay in the courtyard for the night."

The bent figure—it was a woman, Gaius could see now, a young woman—sagged against the man. He strengthened his

support as he said, "My wife. She is about to give birth. There is no room anywhere. Even your court..."

Gaius opened the door wide. "Step in here, please." He took the woman's arm. She felt tense, as if struggling to bear her pain in silence. "The stable will be protected and warm. It is clean. Come. This way."

With the gentleness of a lover, Gaius guided the lady to the stable. The slaves started to attention when they entered, but seeing it was only the innkeeper, they returned to their sleeping positions near their masters' horses. Toward one corner was an empty stall, unused but laid with fresh bedding. As soon as the lady was seated, Gaius became the solicitous host.

"Rest here. I'll return shortly with some blankets and food." He turned away as the young woman bent over to suppress a moan.

He hurried across the court, stopping to bar the door. The sky was clear and brilliant with stars. In the kitchen he roused Anna, the serving girl, to prepare a cold supper of cheese and bread and wine. Then he went to his own rooms.

As he entered, the soft light of a night lamp cast mellow colors on the face of Suzanne. He paused in the doorway. Seeing her lying there in the unguarded trust of sleep, he knew she was worth this life. His love reached out and held her. Her hair was dark against the bedclothes. They rose and fell just perceptibly with her slow breathing. In the muted light he could imagine her as she looked the night after their wedding. He warmed to her,

his beautiful Suzanne. He went to the bed and kissed her closed eyes. She stirred and almost woke.

"Suzanne."

"Oh—Gaius." She smiled through her sleep and caressed him with her eyes. Then she was fully awake and sitting up. "Is anything wrong?

"No, just more people." Before she could reply he hurried on, "But one is a woman, already with the pains of childbirth. She may need your help."

"Where is she? We don't have a corner left."

"I've put them in the stable. It's warm and..."

"The stable! Why, we must let them have this room."

"No, Suzanne. This room will not be taken for any guests. The stable is a fine place. It's warm and clean and quiet. We can make her comfortable in the straw."

Suzanne was already dressing. "I'll take care of the mother. Have you seen to food and light and..."

"Go to the woman, my love. I'll look to the other matters." He took her in his arms. Neither of them was young, but he held her as he had years ago, and the strength of their life together made the years as nothing. She was a good midwife. The woman could have no better help.

Gaius gathered pillows and blankets. He met Anna and told her to bring lights first and then to serve the supper in the stable. He led the way across the court. The sleeping figures did not stir.

Suzanne was bent over the woman talking in low tones. The man stood nearby. He turned to Gaius as the innkeeper approached. "This is very good of you and your wife." The voice was strong but not loud, and Gaius thought he recognized a northern accent.

The innkeeper busily made a pallet of sweet-smelling straw. His wife helped the woman to it. Then he made a bed at a little distance for the man. Anna had returned with food. Gaius served the man, whose eating seemed more out of politeness than hunger. Gaius dismissed the girl with a word to return in an hour.

Child-bearing could take time. He prepared himself for a long night. He glanced at the women. They exchanged whispers. How beautiful my wife is, he thought, bending over that young girl with the confidence and strength of her maturity. No, he thought again, the woman could find no better midwife, even in a palace.

He turned his attention to the man. "Your wife will be fine. It's only too bad the census had to be taken at such a time for her. But Rome doesn't wait for the birth of one child. I dare say, not even for an emperor's child. You are from Galilee?"

"Yes, from Nazareth. But it is right that the child be born here in Bethlehem."

"Bethlehem is a good place. Home of kings. My Suzanne's family have lived here for a long time. They are of the house of David, as is my mother's family. You're here for the census, aren't you?"

"Yes, my wife and I are both descendants of David."

"What work is it that your son—I'm sure it will be a son—will inherit? By the look of your young wife, this must be her first child."

"I am a carpenter. And, yes, this is Mary's first child." He looked to where his wife was reclining.

Gaius was impressed with this younger man's self-possession at the birth of his first child. He seemed to have a sureness beyond his years: not arrogance, but a comfortable maturity. The two men grew silent, each caught away in his own thoughts.

Gaius was again in the hills. The sheep would look like grey rocks on the dark hills. The sky would make him aware of his smallness in the great universe. The companionship of the other shepherds would give him peace in the fire and the human contact they would share.

He thought of his uncle, his mother's brother, who had taken them into his home when his Roman father had gone down with his ship. Belonging to two worlds had its advantages. But somehow, at bottom, he had felt neither Roman nor Jewish. In the cities it sometimes mattered. But never in the hills. And having been once to Rome as a small child with his father, he did not desire the unending stone and constant noise of the bad-smelling cities. Someday… someday.

He was brought back to the present by a moan. The woman Mary was obviously in labor. Suzanne was quiet and efficient in her ministration and encouragement.

Gaius turned to the carpenter. "Let's go outside for awhile."

Reluctantly the man turned and followed Gaius. They stood in the courtyard. It was after midnight and the world was incredibly silent. The stillness felt kinetic, as if a great power held the universe quiet. Time seemed suspended.

Then Suzanne was at his side. "Please, waken Martha and have her come to assist me." She turned to the other man. "Joseph, your son will soon be here. Wait here in the court, until you hear his first cry." She squeezed his arm and then smiled at Gaius before returning to the stable.

Gaius went to the kitchen. The serving girl was sleeping. He roused her to waken Martha, and ordered her to go herself also to aid his wife. Then he returned to his vigil with the man Joseph.

The stars moved west. The silent world slept on. Finally, suddenly, a cry broke the stillness. Joseph turned to the stable door, but did not move toward it. Gaius clapped his shoulders and smiled. "That sounded like a healthy cry. Shall we go see your new son?" And he suddenly realized that everyone had spoken all night as if there had been no doubt that the child would be a son. He smiled ruefully to himself and led the new father to his family.

The dawn showed in the east. Birds had been calling for some time. Gaius, with Suzanne, was crossing the courtyard, which slept in dark shadows, when the knocking sounded. "Go on to bed," he said to his wife. "I'll be with you in a moment."

SOURCES

"Let Nothing You Dismay," by Ruth P. Harnden: from *14 Favorite Christmas Stories,* Scholastic, Inc., edited by Norma Ruedi Ainsworth, © 1964.

"A Father for Christmas," (author unknown): collected and published by Joe L. Wheeler in *Christmas in My Heart, Vol. 2,* Review & Herald Publishing Association, © 1993. Reprinted by permission of the editor-compiler.

"The Christmas Tree," by Mary Austin: from *The Basket Woman: A Book of Fanciful Tales for Children,* by Mary Austin, original © 1904, reprinted in 1969 by AMS Press.

"A Long Way, Indeed," by Arvid Lydecken: excerpted from *Arvilyn Satvja,* by Arvid Lydecken. Excerpt reprinted in *World's Greatest Christmas Stories,* Ziff-Davis Publishing Co., edited by Eric Posselt, © 1949.

"The Tailor's Christmas Guest," by Marcel Brun and Betty Bowen: from *The Shining Tree and Other Christmas Stories,* Alfred A. Knopf, Inc., edited by Hildegarde Hawthorne and Marcel Brun, © 1940.

"Teacher Jensen," by Karin Michaelis: from *A New Christmas Treasury,* Stephen Daye Press, edited by Robert and Maria Lohan, © 1954.

"A Memory of Stalingrad," by Joan Coons: from *A Christmas Treasury,* Viking Penguin, edited by Jack Newcombe, © 1982.

"A Carol for Katrusia," by Annie B. Kerr: from *So Gracious Is the Time,* by Annie B. Kerr, © 1938 by Whiteside, Inc.

"What Amelia Wanted," by Elsie Singmaster: from *Stories to be Read at Christmas,* by Elsie Singmaster, Houghton-Mifflin Co., © 1940.

"To Springvale for Christmas," by Zona Gale: from *The Fireside Book of Christmas Stories,* Bobbs-Merrill, edited by Edward Wagenknecht, © 1945.

"Christmas Eve on Lonesome," by John Fox, Jr.: from *Pearl S. Buck's Book of Christmas,* Simon & Schuster, © 1974. Originally published in 1904.

"A Brand of His Own," by Harry C. Rubicam, Jr.: from *The Shining Tree and Other Christmas Stories,* Alfred A. Knopf, Inc., edited by Hildegarde Hawthorne and Marcel Brun, © 1940.

"I Gotta Idee!" by Elsie Singmaster: from *Stories to be Read at Christmas,* by Elsie Singmaster, Houghton-Mifflin Co., © 1940.

"Which of the Nine?" by Maurus Jókai: from *World's Greatest Christmas Stories,* Ziff-Davis Publishing Co., edited by Eric Posselt, © 1949. Originally published for the first time in English c.1904.

"Christmas in the Cathedral," by Elizabeth Goudge: abridged and excerpted from *The Dean's Watch,* by Elizabeth Goudge. Original © 1960. Reprinted in 1991 by Servant Publications. Used by permission of Servant Publications and the executors of the estate of Elizabeth Goudge.

"The Innkeeper," by Douglas Livingstone: reprinted by permission from *Christianity Today,* December 1, 1978.